I0604033

ALICE K. ARENZ

DARK OF NIGHT

By

ALICE K. ARENZ

Published by Forget Me Not Romances, a division of Winged Publications

ISBN-13: 978-1-0882-1159-5

DEDICATION

For my family—who are patient enough to put up with
me.

ACKNOWLEDGEMENTS

A big thank you to the members of American Christian Fiction Writers who are always willing to answer questions and lend support. I'd also like to thank the awesome KCPD police officer—who prefers to remain anonymous—for taking the time to answer A LOT of questions and giving me a few suggestions along the way.

Writing is a solitary endeavor on many levels, but without the support of an "army" to help you out, we writers would get nowhere. Contrary to popular belief, the internet *does not* have all the answers. If not for the wonderful people in my life who are ready and willing to offer advice and assistance, none of my books would be written. I praise God for you every day.

God bless Cynthia Hickey and Winged Publications. You're my heroes.

Thank you, Lord, for allowing me to live my dream—and for the words to do it.

aka

Chapter 1

"We've got to stop meeting like this, Ms. Carol."

I followed the detective as he weaved through people representing all ages, ethnicities, and walks of life, each of whom had been caught out after curfew. A kind of "controlled" chaos accompanied the din of angry voices and myriad of smells. I preferred the smell of stale perfume and alcohol to that of unwashed bodies, but given the situation...

"Don't you think an eleven o'clock curfew is a little early for the average person?"

"These aren't "average" circumstances." He replied without turning. "You were informed the last time we caught you roaming about—"

"I wasn't roaming. I was on the roof of the Historical Society—with the key Director Hanson provided for access."

"*After* the city-wide curfew."

"Adult curfews have been deemed unconstitu-"

"And I know Hanson told you," he interrupted, ignoring me.

"Just so *you* know, I'd been there since a little before dusk and lost track of the time." It wouldn't matter what I said. This was the second time in as many days that I'd been trotted into the station. I just hoped to get away without an arrest or a fine. I didn't need the hassle. And the thought of having a record... I shivered. Being caught up in the sweep was bad enough.

Well, I hadn't actually been caught in the sweep—not like the rest of the people here. Someone had seen my lantern and reported a peeping Tom.

"It's a good thing there's no access to the roof other than through the building," the detective continued, "Or we wouldn't have contacted Hanson." The scathing glance he threw over his shoulder stilled my retort. Following him without speaking would be hard but probably for the best.

He led me to a small room away from the uproar of the crowd, and I was instantly reminded of old movies and harsh interrogation techniques. Not that this room looked anything like the place where a person would be made to sweat under a hot, glaring spotlight with relentless cops determined to get a confession. To the contrary. The table and chairs looked semi-comfortable, and the lack of a spotlight made it much less daunting than the picture in my head.

My backpack and other totes were at the opposite end of the table from where I stood. I quickly made my way over to them, more concerned about my possessions than the ridiculous idea of being grilled.

Someone had neatly folded my portable easel and collapsible stool, then put them into the appropriate bags. They'd even taken the time to fold the mosquito netting I used to protect my paintings and me from the kamikaze bugs attracted to the special clip-on lamp I used for night painting. The only thing I didn't see was the canvas I'd begun.

"Where's –"

"It was still wet when they brought it in. It's propped against the wall."

I followed the nod of his head and dashed to the canvas.

"Acrylics dry a lot faster than oils, which is why I prefer them." Among the many other reasons not worth sharing. Especially with this detective who appeared intent on making me feel guilty.

I lifted the painting and turned it toward me to check if there'd been any damage. I hadn't gotten far into it, just the night sky with the sliver of moon attempting to highlight the gothic bell tower on the church across the street from my vantage point atop the Society building. There were a few smudges to the lower part of the church that I'd done with a soft lead drawing pencil, but it was nothing I couldn't fix later.

"Are we good?"

I glanced at the detective—I believe Davies was his name—and really looked at him for the first time. I guessed him at around forty, about six feet, 180 to 190 pounds. He had hazel eyes with little flecks of amber that went well with his close-cropped, burnished auburn hair. He didn't flinch under my studied gaze. Probably used to that sort of thing because of his background.

"Well?" The flat tone of his voice was

accompanied by his abrupt manner.

"It's great. Thank you. So, what now?"

"Now, Ms. Carol, I have to find an overworked officer to escort you back to your hotel instead of having him out patrolling the streets where he's needed. There's only two days left of the city-wide curfew. If you're caught out again –"

"You'll throw the book at me."

He helped me gather my things without another word. When he handed me over to the officer waiting to take me back to my room, his stern voice boomed above the rest of the noise in the station, "Make sure she goes directly to her hotel room, and if she gives you any problems, arrest her."

Chapter 2

One month ago, Seaton, Missouri had been given an award as one of the best small cities in which to live—not just in Missouri, but in the entire country. Among the criteria examined was the cost of living, the job market, education, housing and real estate, access to doctors and hospitals, and crime statistics. It had taken the town twenty years to achieve this goal again, and just like twenty years before, no sooner had the stats come out then all hell broke loose. Crimes of all kinds had been on a steady rise. It was almost as if receiving the honor of this award was an invitation to every criminal in the surrounding area to take up residency and cause havoc. It seemed a little coincidental in my mind, but nobody asked my opinion.

My parents were the real artists of the family. Twenty years ago they'd come here not only because of the award but because the diverse architecture was certain to add another depth to the travel book they were compiling on the state. They worked in concert on the photos as well as on the explanations that would chronicle the history of each area and building. Unfortunately, they hadn't lived long enough to finish the book. They'd been murdered on the steps in front of the church I'd been painting tonight.

News of the award stirred something deep in my core, urging me to act. There was unfinished business for me here in Seaton, a call that couldn't be ignored. So, after securing lodging, I contacted my supervisor and put in for vacation time. This shouldn't have been a problem since I'd accrued more than four weeks, but I'd been wrong. The moment my boss discovered where I intended to go, the friction between us began. I guess that's what you get when you are employed by relatives. They knew the history, and they knew me. And rather than fight, I quit.

It wasn't my finest hour, and I really did regret how I'd behaved, but I also knew without a doubt that being here was a necessity. Instead of drawing storyboards for a marketing department, I'd decided to take my love of art to the next level. And where better to start than the city that had so fascinated my parents all those years ago.

Hadley hadn't been happy with my decision but decided not to push the issue any further—as long as I agreed to contact Susan Grady, a friend of the family who lived in Seaton. I'd reluctantly agreed but had yet to follow through. Now, as I sat alone in this oh-so-typical hotel room, staring down at the multiple missed calls from both Hadley and Mrs. Grady, avoidance was no longer an option. I didn't want to worry them.

Despite the late hour, Hadley answered on the first ring, and the tone of her voice made me wish I'd texted instead.

"It's been *three days*, Kelsey, no texts, no calls, no nothing."

"That's a double negative."

"Don't be facetious, young lady. When your parents left you in my care—"

"That was twenty years ago, Aunt Hadley. I'm 32 and perfectly capable of mak—"

"Kelsey."

I hated the stress in her voice and the guilt that came with it. "I apologize. Honestly. It's just been a very busy few days." I crossed my fingers and hoped she didn't know anything about the curfew and sudden crime wave. But, I should have known better.

"Susan told me about the emergency curfew. She also said you hadn't contacted her. We don't even know where you're staying."

"Seaton Inn, right in the heart of downtown, mere blocks away from the police station, about six blocks from the hospital, and there is a church on almost every corner."

"I know you're trying to make light of all this, but you need to understand that we're not taking this trip of yours lightly. It's the first time you've been back to Seaton since your parents were killed. You and I both know that what you really want is to force the police into reopening their case. You'd have better luck making an appeal from home rather than adding to the crisis in their city."

My entire body stiffened as I tried hard to keep my voice from betraying me. "I've been scouting out the city, looking for the best vantage points for my paintings. I haven't approached the police," I gulped at the half truth, "About my parents. Because of the curfew, things are a little tricky."

"Are you persisting in the belief that the only way you can paint is at night?" The tenseness of her voice showed just how worried she was.

"I have no intention of going into dark alleys or becoming anyone's prey. And the night painting—"

"Is the complete opposite of anything your parents would have done. I know. And you know that I love you and don't want anything bad to happen to you."

I started to protest but bit my tongue.

"Promise me you'll give Susan a call first thing in the morning. I know she'd love to have you—she has more than enough room. And you'll be pleasantly surprised by her home."

I gave her my word, then signed off.

Hadley's concern and the hard mattress made my decision an easy one. Independence was all well and good, actually getting a decent night's sleep...

There was no contest. A bed at the Grady house *had* to be better.

Chapter 3

I didn't know much about Susan Grady, just that she'd been my mother's and Aunt Hadley's college roommate and one of their best friends. She was always around at the appropriate times— birthdays, graduation, things like that—usually with her son, Sean, in tow. Susan was a sweet, soft spoken, round little woman with muddy green eyes, always good-natured and polite. Her son, on the other hand, was a loud mouthed, obnoxious bully with a big nose and an even bigger ego. When he'd gone off to college and no longer accompanied his mother on visits, there was no one more thrilled about it than me.

Susan seemed overjoyed when I touched base with her this morning and quickly told me that I was welcome to stay at her place for as long as I wanted.

"I've more than enough room for you," she'd giggled, making me think she had a surprise in store for me. "Lunch is served promptly at 11:45, dear," she'd continued, regaining control. "Do try to get here early."

After giving me directions, she mentioned the time once more before her goodbye. I was curious about the preciseness of lunchtime and hoped the reason behind it wasn't her son. But a free room and a soft bed was enough to strike Sean Grady from my mind.

I gathered my things, inspected the room twice to make sure I had everything, then proceeded to check-out. In no time, I was on my way to the Grady house located just a few miles outside Seaton.

The first part of the journey was easy, a well-marked state highway that was moderately busy. My concern started shortly after making the turn onto the secondary road. Though it was wide and the pavement well-maintained, there were no signs, no markers, and no traffic. Aside from an occasional barn, there were only trees and fields as far as the eye could see. After several miles, I stopped on the shoulder to re-read the directions.

"This has to be right," I assured myself, pulling back onto the roadway.

I hadn't gone far when the county road veered off to the west. It was obvious that the oak-lined lane in front of me was the correct direction to the Gradys' home. When a roof came into view, I assumed it would be one of the many barns that dotted the landscape in rural Missouri. But cresting the hill, my breath was taken away by the sight before me. There was the feeling of having been transported into the English countryside on approach to a stately manor. It brought to mind the romantic suspense novels I'd devoured as a teen, a place the size of a castle with a brooding master and more mystery than was possible to solve.

What I pictured in my mind and reality was

quite different. This wasn't the dark mansion of those long ago books, but a large country house constructed of white stone and light colored bricks. There was a sweeping circular driveway at whose apex was a majestic walkway and a flight of steps that led to the front doors. The place was gorgeous! I already had visions of painting it. Under a full moon would be best, of course, but whatever phase the moon was in, the effect would be awesome.

Other than an enormous six-car garage a discrete distance from the house, there were no other buildings in sight.

I had a strange sense of déjà vu as I drove past the house and parked in front of the garage. An eerie sensation washed over me, causing my arms to erupt in goose bumps.

Had to be the excitement and beauty of the place, nothing more ominous than that.

I left my bags in the car and hoped the walk to the house would calm the butterflies that had made their way from my stomach into my throat. Yet no matter how hard I concentrated on the brilliant redbuds and rows of colorful tulips that lined the drive, the butterflies remained. Even a deep, cleansing breath failed to settle the nervous anticipation that gripped me as I made my way up the grand staircase to the massive wooden double doors. I ran my fingers through my short hair, adjusted my shirt and jeans, and hoped I was presentable enough for the occupants of this fancy house. In the end, it was fascination in the colorful prisms of light from the stained glass insets on either side of the doors that finally calmed my thundering heart. Rainbow colors danced across my hand and arm as I reached toward the doorbell. I may be out of my league but was determined to enjoy every minute of my time here.

I was in the process of removing my sunglasses when the door opened sooner than I'd expected.

"What perfect timing," Susan Grady grabbed hold of my elbow and pulled me inside the large entryway. "You made such good time. I told Fanny that you'd respect her strict meal guidelines. She's, um, a little OCD, but you're going to love her."

It was difficult to concentrate on what Susan was saying while taking in my surroundings. Once again, what I'd expected the house to look like inside was the complete opposite of what it was. It was light and bright without the heavy wood and paneling of a vintage home.

Just off the entryway was a sitting room. Far from the small, intimate size one might have expected, it was more like a living room/great room combined. The walls were painted a soft eggshell, and the woodwork from the crown molding to the baseboards was a pristine white. They were a perfect contrast to the dark walnut floors and the soft beige-colored chairs and sofa. Sunlight poured through large, obviously tinted, windows that were devoid of any coverings.

"You're awfully quiet, Kelsey. I don't remember you ever being this quiet before. In fact, you were quite a chatterbox."

I started to protest then decided she was right. We'd always had a lot of fun during her visits.

"I'm just a little overwhelmed, Mrs. Grady.

Your home is stunning."

"It's Susan, dear. And you're right, it *is* overwhelming." There was a look of pride in her face as her eyes swept over the room. "We've been modernizing the house these last several years. It had been very boxy and horribly dark. We'd like to eventually turn it into a bed and breakfast." She gave me a sweet smile. "One of the rooms we are *very* pleased with is the one you'll be staying in. And you don't have to worry about our schedules. You'll have your own keys to come and go as you please."

I felt like a bobble-head, nodding up and down. Overwhelmed no longer described the magnitude of my befuddled emotions.

I'd no idea Susan had come from money. She'd never seemed to mind our small house and always stayed in our guest room when she visited. Her son had been snooty, but not Susan.

"Thank you so much for your generosity."

"Oh, pooh. We're just glad to have the company. Isn't that right, Fanny?"

I turned around to find a little older version of Susan standing in the doorway.

"You're early. That's good. Come along to the kitchen."

"Fanny, dear, you needn't be in such a big hurry. Please stop for a minute and say hello to our guest. Kelsey, this is my sister Fanny."

"It's actually Frances," she held out her hand. "But I prefer Fanny. Thank you again for your promptness. Lunch is basically ready—just need to get it on the table."

No sooner had she released my hand from her firm grasp than she'd turned and started off down the hall. Susan gave me a slight grimace, shrugged, then motioned for me to follow her sister.

The hallway was wider than any I'd been in before. Evidence of modernizing their home was apparent from the smooth sheet-rocked walls—painted the same eggshell color as the sitting room—to the pristine white of the wainscoting that matched the rest of the woodwork. The flow of the dark hardwood flooring continued long past the doorway into the kitchen.

I think the kitchen was larger than my entire apartment. It was divided in two by an enormous island that accommodated six tall, grey-upholstered bar stools with padded backs. These were lined up neatly on this side of the island, while the opposite side was reserved for prep space. All the countertops had grey and white marbling, probably quartz rather than granite. There were floor to ceiling white Shaker cabinets with brushed nickel handles against one wall, then more cabinets and drawers separated only by what appeared to be oversized stainless steel appliances. Since they appeared a bit darker, I assumed they had a brushed finish—great for hiding fingerprints (thank you HGTV!).

As Fanny made her way into the kitchen proper, Susan took my elbow and directed me to the area that might have been a "breakfast nook" in any other home. Here, it was more the size of a formal dining room!

A huge round table was surrounded by an

enormous bank of bow windows. Sunlight poured in through the slats of plantation shutters, bathing the entire room in soft, filtered light.

There was no need for additional lighting on this bright sunny day, but the modern chandelier above me proved they were prepared for the darkest day. The fixture looked like a conglomeration of styles, one of which seemed more mid-century than anything else. It was suspended above the table by two brushed nickel arms that attached to a rectangular cage made of beveled glass with brushed nickel sides surrounding a row of five Edison bulbs. I'd never seen anything quite like it.

"You look like a deer caught in headlights." Susan giggled. "Try not to be so impressed, dear. It makes me embarrassed." She indicated that I should take a seat. "Now, if you want something to really ooh and ahh about, take a look at this table and chairs. My husband's grandfather built these in the 1800s. From cherry wood, I believe."

"It's all... incredible. Absolutely stunning!"

"And you need to stop being awestruck and eat your lunch." Fanny set a tray on the table that contained a pitcher of iced tea, a large bowl of salad, and smaller bowls of cubed ham, chicken, and beef.

"How about you get things started, Suzy Q, while I take Emma her lunch."

"You've only got three minutes, Sissy. You better skedaddle."

The strange look the sisters exchanged made me uncomfortable. As an odd chill traveled the length of my spine, Susan patted my hand.

"No need to worry, sweetie. That's our mother-in-law."

Chapter 4

Curious, yes. Worried, no. There was a logical explanation; the sisters had married brothers. Though obvious, it *was* unusual—at least to me—and my curiosity increased as we proceeded with our lunch without another mention of the mysterious Emma.

Good food and interesting conversation wiped the chill from the air. The sisters were very talkative, once again sharing their dream of turning the mansion into a bed and breakfast when the renovations were completed.

"Maybe we'll add dinner, too." Susan almost bounced in her chair.

"Might as well make it all meals," Fanny retorted, her sarcasm obvious to me but not to her sister. "I'm already in the kitchen most of the day."

"Wonderful idea!" Susan clapped. "Makes perfect sense to have a full-service inn since we're so far from town. There are so many possibilities."

Fanny rolled her eyes, caught me watching her, and quickly lowered her head to pick at her food. It was close to 12:45 when she excused herself and disappeared without a word. I assumed she was going to retrieve the remains of Emma's lunch.

"She's a real stickler about time."

Susan's remark was barely above a whisper. She dabbed at her mouth with a napkin, then set it aside before rising. "I could lie and say it's her age, but she's always been that way. Never you mind, dear, Emma's peculiarities won't intrude upon your stay. Now," she tapped the table in front of her, "Let's get this cleaned up so Fanny has one less thing she needs to worry about."

It was a little embarrassing to get such a personal insight into the relationship with her mother-in-law. To avoid any further awkwardness—on my part, anyway—I jumped up and lent a hand to clear away the dishes.

"Glad you're not like most people these days, constantly on their cell phones." Susan said as she loaded the dishwasher. "Why, Sean can't seem to live without checking his every second."

I laughed. "Seems to be the "in" thing to do these days. Technology is great, but feeling you have to be "available" all the time, well, to be honest, it's intrusive. My cell is off most of the time."

"That seems the sensible thing to do—"

"Not very practical, however. One never knows when an emergency might arise. You wouldn't want to waste time turning on the phone and having to wait for it to go through its gyrations when you need it immediately." Fanny set Emma's tray on the counter and shooed Susan and me away. "I'll admit to being irritated at times, but I do love the convenience." She wiped her hands on a towel. "Why don't you take Kelsey up to her room? I'm sure she has more important things to do than hanging around a couple old ladies."

I was prepared to protest, to remind them they were Hadley's age, when Susan took me by the hand and led me out of the kitchen.

"I don't consider you old at all."

"That's sweet, dear. Why, the mid-fifties today is the new thirty. Or something like that, for goodness sake. But it doesn't do any good to argue with her when she gets in a mood. I'm surprised she didn't give us one of her lectures on the joys of the modern age." Susan smirked. "Come along, dear, your room is the first one at the top of the stairs. And the only one completely remodeled."

The staircase, which was just to the left of the front doors, seemed to rise organically out of the foyer. It made a graceful arc before climbing to the second-floor landing.

"We left the wood just as it was rather than painting it out. It was all hand-carved by our husbands and their father."

There it was again, the reference of "our." Made me want to know the details even if it wasn't my business.

"We had to paint the wainscoting so that it matched what we'd done on the first floor." Susan continued, appearing to caress the handrail as we made our way up the stairs. "But it turned out well in the end.

"Now, your room is a bit smaller than some of the others, but it's nicely proportioned. It has a queen-sized bed, a reading nook, dressers, and, of course, its own bathroom. Plus," she giggled, "a surprise I'm sure you'll appreciate." She grinned at me over her shoulder. "We have WiFi, but you'll have to wait until Sean comes by to get you fixed up. That's one thing Fanny has yet to figure out."

"Not a problem." I'd barely gotten the words out when she pushed open the door and, with a little flourish of her hand, presented the room to me.

"Don't you just love this color of grey? It picks up on the colors around it which adds so much more interest, don't you think?" She didn't wait for an answer. "We're using it in all the guest rooms, though each will have a different theme color. As you can see, yours is in various shades of blue. Like a little slice of heaven."

"It's gorgeous." And that was an understatement. From the darkest midnight to the lightest pastel, everything was tastefully coordinated. If you were partial to blue, this was the room you'd want.

"It was difficult, but we eventually found a place to supply the cushy mattresses we wanted. I don't know why these companies think we all want to sleep on a sheet of plywood." She shook her head. "Not everyone wants a hard bed, for goodness sake. And when they say "pillow top," I believe it should be a deep cushion you can sink into. Sheesh."

"Uh huh." Sounded good to me. Especially after the last few nights on said "sheet of plywood."

I'd just started to become acclimated to my incredible surroundings when I was awestruck once more. Spacious, comfortable, welcoming—there weren't enough adjectives to describe it.

"Two closets?"

"One, dear." There it was again, that little giggle accompanied by a mischievous expression. "That's the closet," she said, pointing to the door near the bathroom entrance. "This one's a surprise." Susan strode across the room to throw open the door next to the reading nook that included a comfy-looking window seat and expansive window. "Come along, Kelsey." She winked at me before reaching inside the dark void. A light came on revealing a narrow staircase.

"This used to be an entrance to the attic. Now, it gives direct access to what they used to call a widow's walk. It's more like a small rooftop deck."

The moment I stepped out onto the deck, I knew why Susan had been so excited about her "surprise."

"What a wonderful view!" There were miles of fields—pastureland?—I wasn't really sure. Not corn or soybeans, that much I knew. There were rolling hills flanked by stands of trees. Beautiful but also haunting with its vast emptiness.

"If you look straight out there, just to your right, you'll see a little knoll dotted by a few maples. That's where the old house was located. We've cleaned it up, but bits of the foundation remain so it'd be best for you to stay away from the area. Not that you'd want to go there anyway," she added quickly. "We have a lovely garden with a little brook running through it. Why, we even have a footbridge. And with all the spring flowers in bloom... You'll love it!"

I nodded my agreement as I traversed the

circumference of the deck, peering over the peaks of the roof, examining everything that might provide another dimension to possible future paintings. That's when I spotted the flat area on the roof of the garage. It would have a perfect view of the house, exactly what I'd envisioned earlier.

"What about that area on the garage?"

"Oh, well, I'd have to ask about it, of course. But I know why you'd like to set up there." Her smile wavered, her voice hesitant. "I'll have to get back to you, dear. You do understand, don't you? We're not all as open as perhaps we should be."

After the leisurely way she'd introduced me to her home, I had the sudden impression that I wasn't as welcome here as she'd wanted me to believe. It was an odd thought. But as she ushered me off the deck and back to my room, the giggling, mischievous woman seemed to disappear, replaced by someone eager to be on her way.

"Now you know your way around, feel free to come and go as you please." She dug in her pocket and pulled out a couple of keys. "The square-topped one is for the front door, the round for your room. Fanny will set out a buffet for dinner a little before six. It'll be up till seven. You're welcome to come any time you want, eat in the kitchen, outdoors, or bring it up here if it makes you more comfortable. Just make yourself at home." She scooted to the door so quickly I barely had the time to say a heartfelt thank you. She waved it away, began closing the door, then popped her head back inside.

"Do stay away from the garage for now, except to get things from your car, of course. It just won't do for you to get into a place you don't belong… er, without proper permission."

"I promise."

"And I'll hold you to that promise." She shut the door, leaving me to wonder exactly what had just happened.

24

Chapter 5

"So, have you gotten settled in?" There was definite relief in Hadley's voice.

"Not exactly. My things are still in the car. To be honest, I'm not sure I'm wanted here." I related what had happened since my arrival and how Susan and her sister had run hot and cold, giving me mixed signals.

"Susan's always been a little flighty, but it's nothing to be concerned about. Look, kiddo, the moment I told her you were headed to Seaton, she was adamant that you should stay with her. And I don't think it's just because she knew it would put me more at ease. She's a peacemaker, Kels, and probably trying to tread that fine line between what she wants and what the rest of the family feels comfortable with. I don't know Fanny well and admit she's a bit more reserved than Susan but still very welcoming. I know she bears the majority of the burden of caring for their mother-in-law, so maybe she was having a bad day. Susan assured me that everyone was on board with you staying there." Hadley gave a little laugh. "She's a real character, kept your mother and me in stitches. We really missed her when she dropped out of college."

From all the stories, I'd assumed they'd roomed together all four years. Not that it mattered.

"The house and grounds are wonderful, and they really have been nice. It's just… I don't want to be in the way."

"From my impression of Fanny, if she didn't want you around, you wouldn't be there. So, quit worrying, and try to enjoy your surroundings. It's not every day you get the chance to stay in a fancy country manor. And it really does make me feel better to know you're out of Seaton and away from the temptation of going out during the curfew."

"Which ends tomorrow." I added, ready to change the subject. "So, the sisters married brothers."

"Did I forget to mention that? Sorry, Kels. It wasn't topmost in my mind. Keeping you out of trouble was."

I knew if we continued the conversation it was sure to go in a direction I didn't want to discuss. By the time we hung up, Hadley was reassured of my safety, and I felt a lot better about staying at the Grady house.

~~~

The warmth of the sun felt good after the slight chill in the house. It was funny, but until I'd come outside, I hadn't even realized the chill had been a real thing and not just a result of the seeming flip-flop of Susan's attitude. I was determined to shrug it off and believe my aunt's friend genuinely wanted me in her home.
~~~

The trees and bushes whispered in the warm breeze, reminding me that spring was here with all its glorious trappings.

It also reinforced the fact that yesterday was the anniversary of my parents' murders.

April had been a rough month for me these last twenty years. The contrast between the reawakening of life that springtime brought, and the deaths of my parents, had been difficult to reconcile. My enthusiasm in watching tulips, crocuses, hyacinths, and daffodils burgeoning from the sleepy ground dampened the closer we came to April 28th. And though I'd long since learned to deal with the occasional nightmares that returned during this time, I'd never quite managed to put the past into proper perspective and move forward. Hadley knew this, which is why she'd been so concerned about me coming here—*being* here. But things were about to change, I'd felt it the moment I'd learned about the award… the instant I'd read the latest column in *The Seaton News* pertaining to my parents' case. This would be the last spring of feeling so lost and conflicted.

I'd been so deep in thought I hadn't noticed another car parked next to mine. The fire engine red Mustang convertible made my poor eighteen-year-old Protégé look older and more run down than it really was.

"Kelsey Carol," the owner of the rich baritone voice popped up from the other side of my vehicle. "I thought this looked like your Aunt Hadley's old car." He patted the roof. "I've fond memories of this vehicle."

"Excuse me?" That was a peculiar statement. And who... "Sean?" I barely recognized the tall, nice-looking man, had trouble relating him to the pesky kid who used to torment me.

"It's been what, six, seven years?" He came toward me with his hand outstretched.

"More like ten," I answered, shaking his hand. "College graduation. Mine, not yours. I don't believe we were invited to that."

"Because I didn't go. All that pomp and circumstance and fawning over the act of getting a degree… I was just happy it was over so I could get on with my real life. Sorry, no offense intended."

I knew that wasn't true, but hey, I was willing to give him the benefit of the doubt. Especially after he offered to help me get my stuff up to my room.

I stole a sidelong glance at him as he climbed into my car. He was a little over six feet, slender, with dark brown hair and pale blue eyes. He'd grown into his nose, which was remarkable in itself. Made me wonder if he'd grown out of his big ego and propensity to bully.

"I'm guessing they put you in the blue room since it's the one with deck access."

"Susan said it was the only one completely finished, though she did seem excited about me using the deck to paint."

"You still prefer to paint at night?"

I nodded. "It's a different world then. Purer somehow." I didn't expect him to understand when no one else ever had.

"I get it. Probably makes it easier to concentrate when there's no one around to bug you."

"Except the bugs." We both laughed.

"And you're not afraid of being alone?"

Was this some kind of test? If it was, I wasn't about to fail.

"You'd be surprised by what a well-placed knee and a sturdy easel can do. So no, I'm not afraid of being out alone."

"Good for you! The only other thing I'd recommend is a Taser—just in case the first two things don't work."

"Thanks for the suggestion. I'll look into it. I'm surprised Hadley hasn't mentioned getting one."

Without a single complaint, he helped me get everything up to my room—carrying the bulk of it. I was pretty sure the old Sean Grady wouldn't have been as helpful.

"Let me know if you need anything. I'll be happy to lend a hand." He set the last of my bags on a luggage rack then stood staring at me. "I'd always liked your long hair, Kelsey. Reminded me of *Alice in Wonderland*. Too bad you cut it."

"Um, thanks, I guess." I had to fight that girlie thing of fiddling with my hair. Strange that the more you tried to avoid doing something, the greater the impulse became. Better to change the subject.

"By the way," I said, my hands tucked securely in my pockets. "Have you finished the novel you insisted you were going to write?"

"The elusive "great American novel" every writer wants to publish. Not yet, but I'm working on it. All it needs is the end, which is proving to be the toughest part of the whole thing. What about you, Kelsey, have you decided whether or not you're an artist or an ad exec?"

"Not an executive. And it's marketing." My eyes met his in the challenge I was certain he'd issued. "I guess the jury's still out on that one. We'll have to see how things work out."

He smiled. "I've got a feeling you're going to do just fine Kelsey Carol." He glanced down at his watch. "Look, I've gotta go. My grandmother's waiting for me"

He was almost out the door when I remembered the WiFi.

"I've written down the instructions and showed both of them how to reconnect, but, for some reason, they just don't seem to get it."

That didn't sound like Fanny—his mom, but not Fanny. She seemed the type to be on top of all things technical.

"I'll get you set up before I leave," he promised. "Right now, Emma's expecting me, and I don't like to keep her waiting."

Chapter 6

It had been a surprisingly pleasant encounter. Perhaps Sean had grown up after all.

Maybe we both had.

I took advantage of all the storage provided and actually unpacked. By the time I was finished with my clothes and essentials, only one bag remained. I pulled it onto the bed—which was *very* comfortable—piled the pillows against the headboard and prepared myself for the next step.

It was always the same, the deep intake of a fortifying breath, a moment of prayer with my eyes tightly shut, and the slight hesitation as my fingers flipped open the latch. Raising the lid of the case revealed the large 3-ring binder and folders that comprised the history of my parents' murders.

COUPLE MURDERED IN WEE HOURS OF MORNING IN FRONT OF ST. ANDREW'S CHURCH, yelled the initial headline followed by the gruesome details of how they'd been gunned down within minutes of *The Seaton News* delivery truck passing by on its early morning run to fill their vending machines.

I flipped past years of stories—knew them all by heart—until I got to the ones from the last five years. That's when S. Pattison had taken up the crusade, calling for the investigation to be reopened and issuing a challenge to the Missouri Attorney General to get involved. But even when state investigators stepped in the void, "the lack of leads" left the case as cold as it was on the day the crime had been committed.

"Another anniversary of the murders of Miles and Payton Carol has come, yet we're no closer to discovering and prosecuting the perpetrator than we were twenty years ago. It's time, no, past *time to give the family justice for this heinous crime.*

Imagine coming to Seaton for the sole purpose of highlighting the city in a book you're preparing on your beloved state. You're taking photos and gathering the history of each place you visit. Your motive is innocent, pure—so much so that you've brought along your family to add to the enjoyment of your working vacation. That's what happened, folks, why the Carols were in Seaton that fateful morning. It's only by the grace of God their young daughter wasn't with them on the steps of St. Andrew's when their lives were cut short by a burst of gunfire.

The initial investigation and canvass of the area came up with nothing. Other than the newspaper delivery driver's report to police, no one else came forward. The seeming lack of clues relegated the case into cold status almost immediately. But it doesn't have to remain that way. With your help and today's technology, this mystery can be solved. Someone somewhere has an answer, a clue that will blow this investigation wide open.

So, once again, I call on you. If you have any information, no matter how small or insignificant you might think it is, now is the time to speak out. If you feel uncomfortable talking to the local cops, call the following number and speak with state investigators. Or, you can always contact me here at the paper. Remain anonymous if you feel the need, but don't let another year go by leaving Payton's daughter and sister without answers."

"By the grace of God." I reread the words, trying to understand why they nudged at the corner of my mind, like an itch I couldn't quite reach. Better to concentrate on what I knew instead of searching for memories that weren't there. And I knew I needed to meet this person. To date, however, all my calls, emails, and letters had remained unanswered. Inquiries made directly to the managing editor were met with apologies and the assurance that the columnist had received all my messages. I refused to accept his word... especially after reading this last column. I wanted a face-to-face, nearly demanded their cooperation, but was once again put off by the pat answer that S. Pattison would get back to me at "their earliest convenience." It had been four days, and there was still no response.

I packed up the collection, placing everything back inside the leather attaché that had once belonged to my dad. My fingers lingered on the raised brass letters of his initials, and though my throat tightened and tears lurked at the corners of my eyes, I refused to give in to the onslaught of emotions.

I'd been waiting twenty years for answers that had never come. Whenever asked, Hadley would reassure me that everything that could be done to solve the case was being done, that I had to be patient and let the professionals handle it. As much as I loved my aunt, this was an area where we disagreed. Where she trusted, I doubted, wondering if perhaps she'd pushed a little harder...

No, that was wrong. I shouldn't blame Hadley or criticize her faith in the police. She truly believed God would provide them the clues needed to resolve the case. Though my conviction in God was strong, it didn't extend to the cops. It had been too long to expect any more than the same. Hadley would call that "stinking thinking," and remind me that our prayers for justice would be answered. She was right; I knew that deep down, but it was difficult to accept.

I shoved my back into the headboard, hitting my head in the process. A contrite "sorry" aimed heavenward was all I could muster.

It wasn't just me who needed the case solved—S. Pattison was proof of that. As the column stated, Hadley was right there with me. She'd picked up the pieces of our lives, moving us beyond the tragedy the best she could. It hadn't been easy for her to lose her twin any more than it had been for me to lose both mother and father. We'd stood together, though not always on the same page, but together nonetheless.

I wasn't about to simply sit around when I could be out there working to get answers. I was done waiting.

And the best place to start would be with the mysterious S. Pattison.

36

Chapter 7

There was still plenty of time to go back into Seaton to visit the newspaper office. Perhaps being a little more forceful by going to his place of work would convince S. Pattison to finally talk with me. I didn't plan on making a scene, but maybe it would be a good idea to remind everyone of how badly it would look for him to continue avoiding me.

Him. I didn't even know whether S. Pattison was male or female!

After setting my laptop on a table near the door, I jotted off a quick note to Sean, thanking him in advance for getting me set up on the family's network. I made sure the note would be clearly seen when he approached my room, tucking it into the closed door just above the handle—leaving the room unlocked. As tightly as the door closed, I was certain the paper would stay in place.

Within twenty minutes I was at the reception desk of the newspaper office. After several go-rounds with the receptionist, she did as I'd first suggested and called the managing editor to come speak with me. I'd expected to be taken to his office and eventually introduced to S. Pattison. It didn't happen.

"I assure you, Miss Carol, S. Pattison has received every message you've left—in their various forms." The balding little man in front of me crossed his arms and frowned. "You have to be patient. He'll get back to you in due time."

"Him?" I jumped on the pronoun—it was either that or jumping all over the guy for the "patient" and "due time" remarks. "So the author of the columns is a man?"

"We can neither confirm nor deny that conjecture. The individual is relying on us for our discretion and prefers to remain anonymous at this time."

"Mr. Woods," I flashed him my friendliest smile, but while it might work on some people, it certainly didn't faze him. "Look, I'm not trying to break into the Watergate and steal your secrets. I'm simply attempting to contact the person responsible for the recent columns about my parents' murders-"

"I understand."

"Then you can surely understand why I'm here, why I'd like the opportunity to speak with this guy/woman who's supporting the drive for a new investigation."

Woods didn't budge. If anything, his stance became firmer, his expression harder.

"As you know, there has been a great deal of controversy surrounding the mystery of the murders. At this time—"

"Are you implying that you're protecting the individual's identity because they're undercover?"

"I'm neither implying nor inferring, Miss Carol, just stating facts. Now, if you'll excuse me, I need to get back to work." He turned on his heal and left the reception area.

The young woman behind the desk offered me a notepad and pen, but I ignored her. She and Woods both stated that S. Pattison had received all my messages. I doubted one more would make a difference.

Frustrated, I slammed the door of the newspaper office behind me—or would have if it hadn't been designed to close so slowly it was impossible to slam. I did, however, run headlong into the person passing by on the sidewalk. The man's quick response kept us from toppling over.

"Ms. Carol? It's Adam Davies." The detective steadied me with firm hands on both of my shoulders.

"Sorry. I mean thanks." The sun caused the amber flecks in his eyes to sparkle. A weird thing to notice under the circumstances. "Guess I should have been more careful."

"Are you ok? You look a little frazzled."

What an odd choice of word, though it did describe how I felt. Still, I certainly didn't need the cop who'd basically been hassling me to tell me how I looked.

"I'm fine. Really. So you can let go now."

"As long as you're sure." He removed his hands. "I was on my way to the coffee shop up the street. You're welcome to come if you'd like."

I couldn't help being suspicious of his conciliatory attitude and concerned expression. After all, he'd wanted to throw me in jail last night.

"Is the invitation official business, Detective?"

"Not at all. Just being neighborly, ma'am," he said with a fake country drawl and exaggerated smile. "Seriously, Ms., uh, Kelsey, I thought you might need someone to talk to."

Talk? I wasn't sure he was the right person for me to share my frustrations. He *was,* however, among the people I wanted to speak to.

"If the place has iced tea, I'm in."

Joe & Dough was a short two blocks away. It shouldn't have been a surprise that the "coffee shop" also sold doughnuts.

"I see that smirk on your face," Davies grinned at me. "I don't come here for the doughnuts. I come for the best darn coffee in the city. It doesn't hurt that the doughnuts are good, too."

They may have the best coffee in town, but I was sure their iced tea was every bit as good. As for the doughnuts… they were definitely not something my diet needed. Or my waistline.

"So, the emergency curfew ends tomorrow?" I waited while he lingered over his bite of apple fritter. "You have the city back under control?"

Davies took a swallow of his coffee, wiped his mouth with a napkin, then set down the cup with deliberation. "The city was never out of our control. And yes, the curfew ends tomorrow at midnight. I hope that doesn't mean you'll be out at 12:01 atop one of our buildings. Do us all a favor and wait a couple days."

"Tell you what, how about a deal?" I pushed my plate to the side and folded my hands on the table in front of me. "I'll do as you suggest and stay off the rooftops for a day or two if you agree to answer a few questions about my parents' case."

"I don't make deals, especially one like that. As for answering your questions, that depends. You know there's a limited amount of information that can be released in an ongoing investigation. I can understand how the columns in *The Seaton News* could cause you to question everything the police have done, or not done, in the last twenty years. Rest assured that this case has never been far from any of our minds."

"That's good to know, of course, but I've always been curious about some things and it would be nice to get real answers rather than being put off or ignored. And trying to placate me with words that don't really mean anything isn't going to work. Look," I drew in a deep breath. "I know that there are cameras inside and outside nearly every building and that law enforcement has the ability to access the footage. I've even seen how cases have been solved by tracking victims and suspects from one camera to another. You guys piece the info together to help establish alibis and discover hidden clues."

"That's true, but you're talking twenty years ago." He shifted in his seat, almost glaring at me. "I'm sure you already know about the two cameras on the Historical Society's building at that time."

I nodded. "One faced toward the entrance, the other on the parking lot. I also know that the cameras on the bank a couple blocks down didn't have a view of St. Andrew's." His expression seemed to intensify. But if he was expecting me to back down, he was going to be sadly disappointed.

"Adam, I hope you don't mind me calling you that," a slight incline of his head encouraged me to continue. "As far as I know, you found nothing on CCTV video from the area that could help. But what about their cell phones? Did you subpoena the records, track their movements from the tower pings? Was that even possible then?" He didn't answer, just remained silent and stoic. "The vast amount of information that can and could be accessed blows my mind. Yet, it's impossible to even guess what your department has or hasn't done."

"Is that all?" His tone was far from congenial. I needed to find a way to win him back, regain that sign of friendship he'd extended earlier.

"I'm sorry if you think I'm criticizing the way the investigation's been handled. I'm not, truly. You've got to understand how maddening this is."

"Are we through?"

He looked like he was ready to leave. I couldn't let that happen. Not yet.

"Adam, please wait. I was upset about how they treated me at the newspaper, and I've taken it out on you. I apologize. There really are a couple questions I'd like to ask if you'd give me a little more of your time."

"No more tirades?" Though I hadn't thought of it that way, I wasn't about to argue with him.

"No more. Promise." I guess I was properly contrite because he gave me the go-ahead to continue.

"My parents always took two to four cameras with them on shoots. All I've got from their time here is one of the 35mm's and a couple rolls of film. I assume the police would have put everything found with my parents into evidence, but I've always wondered the whereabouts of their favorite cameras. I've asked my aunt, but any mention of the murders upsets her so much she changes the subject. Would you be able to check into this for me?"

"I know there is a camera and film in the evidence box. That's all I can say. And you're right, everything they had with them on the scene would have been protected and preserved."

I took a sip of my tea and tried to keep my hands from trembling. I knew the strap of one of the cameras had been around my mother's neck—I'd seen a photo in the newspaper before Aunt Hadley had the chance to destroy it. Try as I might to find that picture again, I'd been unable to do so. And I'd checked newspaper archives from various cities throughout the state.

"If you only have one camera in evidence then there could be at least two that are missing, as well as several rolls of film. They'd left the camera I have in the place they were staying."

"I'm sure you're aware that investigators would have gone through their room with a fine toothed comb. To be honest, I'm surprised they released those things to your aunt. If I'd been in charge, everything would still be in evidence. You never know where clues might come from."

He moved his chair slightly away from the table, leaned back, and crossed his legs. "You know, I hadn't been on the force very long when your parents came to town. I was assigned as an escort on some of their shoots. Not for protection, but to assist them with documentation at some of the sites. I've always been fascinated in the area's history, and the captain thought I was a good choice to help them out."

"That's… interesting."

"Frankly, I'm surprised you don't remember me."

"Remember you?" If he was trying to throw me off balance, he'd succeeded. I could feel my mouth hanging open and was forced to close it by "nonchalantly" placing my hands beneath my chin. It didn't fool him. The odd glint in his eyes and smug expression told me he had me exactly where he wanted—out of kilter and tongue-tied. While I attempted to rack my brain for a memory I was certain I didn't possess, his amusement with my sudden confusion was obvious.

Yes, Hadley and I had come to Seaton after the murders, but there was something in his behavior that caused me to doubt myself.

"You remind me a lot of your mother. She had the same sort of drive and determination."

I stared at him long and hard. "I thought you only accompanied my parents on a few shoots." It took a lot of resolve, but my voice was strong, steady.

"A true statement, Ms. Carol. But you're forgetting that I'm a detective trained in reading people."

"A profiler?

He shrugged. "In effect. Would you like to

know how I read you?"

"I'm fairly certain I already know: 'A nuisance with more curiosity than brains.' Am I right?"

"Pretty much," he laughed. "I don't blame you, Kelsey, but I do want to caution you. Remember, you're not a cop and have no idea what you might come up against."

"Better to be safe." I mimicked what I'd heard too many times in the past.

"You got it. By the way, I called the inn this morning to check on you. They told me you'd checked out."

"Uh, yeah." Focus, focus. "I'm staying with some old family friends. The Gradys, just west of town."

"I know them. The family has lived here since the city was founded. At one time, they owned the largest farm in this part of the state. Later, they got into construction and real estate. Why, Grady Brothers Construction has been one of the biggest companies in the area for decades."

"Ah." So that's where the money came from. "Susan Grady went to college with my mom and aunt. She and Sean visited a lot when I was a kid. That's all I really know about the family."

He raised his eyebrows in what I interpreted as surprise. I guess it was unusual not to know at least a little something more about the family, but it had never come up. Until now. My curiosity was piqued.

"Sean Grady has always been a bit of a troublemaker." He remarked, standing abruptly. "I'd be careful around him."

"Thanks for the warning, Detective. I'll keep it in mind."

Chapter 8

Detective Davies had given me a lot to think about. The problem with my entire visit to Seaton this afternoon was that I came away with more questions than answers. I never liked the saying of taking one step forward and multiple steps backward, but that's exactly how I felt. It didn't make me happy, only frustrated and more determined than ever to discover the truth.

The drive back to the Grady house was grueling. Facing the sun was only half the battle, feeling the tell-tale signs of a migraine made it worse. By the time the house came into view, my head was pounding, and all I wanted to do was get some medicine and lie down. A migraine of monumental proportions had a tight hold on me.

Pulling into the circle drive, I noticed Sean's car was gone. I wondered if that meant he didn't live here. Though I didn't see anyone outside or inside, the sound of distant voices assured me I was not alone.

I trudged up the staircase, praying no one heard me come in. I was quickly becoming less and less functional. Making polite conversation would be next to impossible, and I had no desire to offend my hosts by refusing to show them consideration.

The note was gone from my door and placed atop my computer on the table where I'd left it. A glance revealed a message from Sean had been added at the bottom of the original note, but because of the way I felt, it would have to wait till later.

I didn't get migraines often, but when I did, the only real remedy was to lie down in a dark, quiet room until it was gone. The last few days had created a perfect storm: lack of sleep, too many stressors, and way too much input.

I rushed straight to the bathroom where I'd left my meds, downing them in such haste that half the water ended up on my t-shirt. Under other circumstances I might have cared enough to at least remove the shirt, but not today.

I quickly shut the blinds and pulled the heavy drapes across both windows. When light from the bathroom window pierced the darkened room, that door was closed. I carefully navigated my way to the bottom of the bed, then crawled up to the head and tugged at the spread. Unable to find the opening between the sheets, I pulled at the excess bedding that hung over the side and covered myself as best I could. By the time my head hit the pillows, I was spent. Closing my eyes, images of the crime scene burned my retinas.

My parents *would* get justice. Just not today.

~~~

What were those lights and eerie figures that seemed to hover above the ground? At this distance
~~~

I couldn't be sure what I was seeing, but it wasn't normal—not at three in the morning, or any other time.

I kept my flashlight off not wanting the "ghosts" to realize they were being observed. Should I continue to watch or return to bed? I was torn between curiosity and terror. The terror won out when it appeared the beings were coming closer. I had to protect myself and my parents…

I sprang up from the bed, ringing wet from sweat, still shaking from a nightmare I hadn't had in years. It took a few minutes to acclimate to my surroundings; the Grady house. I was in Seaton at Susan Grady's home in the fabulous blue room.

I reached to the side of the bed where I remembered a lamp sitting on the night table. One click and darkness was dispelled to the far reaches of the room. Able to tolerate the low wattage without pain, I tried a second click. It was enough to show the entire room, chasing away all doubt that it was anything more than a nightmare.

I checked my watch, almost shocked by the time: 2 a.m.

I'd gotten back to the house around five and gone to bed shortly thereafter, which meant I'd been asleep for over eight hours. The benefit to that was the migraine was gone, and I felt a lot better. The only downside was being hungry. It probably wasn't the best idea to wander through the house in the middle of the night and risk disturbing someone. It would be better to settle on some of the chocolate covered mints I kept on hand for late night hunger attacks after painting for hours.

I got a glass of water from the bathroom and while munching on my third mint, spied the note Sean had left.

"You're all set up with WiFi. Let me know if you have any problems. I look forward to seeing you again. Sean."

It was a nice, innocuous message. Not worthy of the warning Detective Davies had given me. Besides, I already knew a little about Sean Grady from when we were kids. I didn't need any more warning than that. There was always the possibility he'd grown out of his bad behavior even as he had grown into his nose.

I took the laptop to the writing desk, pleased by the strong internet signal. It was time to find out a little more about the people I was staying with.

There was more information on Grady Brothers Construction than I would have imagined—including a website dedicated entirely to the history of the company.

Grady Brothers Construction originally began as Grady & Sons Woodworking at the turn of the 20th Century. The founder, Matthew Grady, who preferred woodworking over farming, sold half the family farm and used the capital to establish the new company. He was known for his affordable and well-crafted furniture that graced nearly every home in this part of Missouri. His younger sons, Elijah and Micah, joined him in the business, setting a new standard of excellence with their carpentry. Noah, the elder son, continued to work on what was left of the family farm until his untimely death from an accident that also claimed the lives of his wife and daughter.

By 1945, only Elijah remained of the original brothers. He leased most of the remaining farmland and concentrated on carpentry. His son, Luke, whose specialty was in general construction, added another dimension to the business.

The family tradition continued when Luke's sons, Saul and Caleb, joined the company in 1972. After their father's death, they changed the name to Grady Brothers Construction.

Tragedy struck the Gradys once more when a car accident in 2016 took the lives of the brothers. Though they are no longer with us, their mother Emma, ensures their spirits remain the driving force behind the current company.

A little wordy, but it put things in perspective.

The web page went on to mention the marriages of Caleb and Saul to sisters Fanny and Susan Lane. I was puzzled there wasn't any mention of Sean. It wasn't until I went onto a different site that Sean's name was mentioned as having taken a totally different path. The author made the statement that while the Grady family had made their fortune in farming, construction, and real estate, the only remaining descendant, Sean Grady, was more interested in "writing" than in the family tradition. The article didn't mention an author, and its very anonymity made the catty remark about Sean seem more spiteful than unbiased reporting. As a matter of fact, it sounded like someone who was jealous or had an axe to grind.

Another link that mentioned Sean referred to him as a "two-bit hack whose interests lay in womanizing and living off family money instead of hard work and integrity."

It was apparent Sean had stepped on someone's toes—several someones by the look of it. And though the stories continued to get worse, I followed yet another link that questioned how the Gradys managed to make so much money during the Depression. Despite the doubters, it was obvious there were just as many people who considered them to be a wonderful and industrious family who always looked out for their community.

I didn't find a Facebook page for Sean, which I found curious, but he was on *The Seaton News'* website. They seemed to like him there.

While on the paper's site, I checked for information about the accident that had taken the lives of the Grady brothers in 2016. *The Seaton News* had covered it extensively. I chose one article from a few days after the incident had been reported.

Witnesses saw the truck suddenly veer off the highway and careen down the embankment into the river. Despite the massive effort of several departments across the state, neither Saul's nor Caleb's bodies have been found. The original belief that they'd not only made it out of the truck and survived the ordeal no longer seems a possibility. A source states that the search and rescue operation has changed to one of recovery. But with the rapidly moving currents in this part

of the Missouri, the chance of finding their bodies is uncertain.

"The poor family!" The sound of my voice gave me a little jolt. For some reason, I looked around the room. "There's no one here, dummy," I giggled.

Out of curiosity, I looked up Detective Davies. The website for the city's police department referred to him as "a decorated police officer and detective whose service has made him one of Seaton's most valuable public servants, earning him the respect of all who know him." There were also several articles that reiterated how his dedication to his job and the citizens of his hometown made him a favorite of the community. One even stated that Missouri historians valued Davies's vast knowledge of Seaton and the surrounding area.

Talk about comparing a sinner and a saint. I was sure if I looked hard enough I'd eventually find articles that appreciated Sean's contribution to society. One would hope, anyway.

I got up from the desk and stretched. There was brief consideration of dashing off a note to Hadley, but I decided against it. As much as I wanted her take on Detective Davies's remark about my "knowing" him, I didn't want to worry her. She knew that only a migraine would have caused me to end up on the computer in the middle of the night. If I'd been feeling well, I'd have been too busy painting to even consider being online.

I closed the laptop, weighing my options. I could set up my equipment on the deck, but it was a little late to get started on anything. And though I was still tired and the comfy bed called to me, I didn't really want to chance lying awake for hours tossing and turning. That's when it hit me. I didn't have to use the deck for painting alone. There were, after all, chairs set up so one could enjoy the atmosphere.

I drew back the drapes and peeked out of the blinds. It was a clear night, the kind that was good for stargazing. I grabbed a flashlight out of my backpack, pulled on a jacket, and snatched a small blanket off the window seat. The cool night air was just what was needed before returning to bed.

I checked the door to the deck twice to make sure it wasn't locked. Positive there'd be no difficulty getting back to my room, I closed the door, leaving the light on in the stairwell.

It was a bit colder than I'd expected. I hugged my jacket around me, glad I'd thought to bring along the throw. Snuggling onto the deeply padded chaise lounge, I pulled the blanket over me and gazed into the heavens.

The sky seemed clearer because of the chill, causing the stars to glisten with a clarity you could only get away from city lights. There was a waning crescent moon that emitted very little light, but between it and the stars, there was more than enough for me. I stuck the flashlight into my pocket, drew in a deep breath, held it for a moment with closed eyes, then breathed out at the same time I opened my eyes to glory in the beauty of my surroundings.

A sudden, unexpected sound broke the silence, reverberating in the stillness for a few seconds before dissipating. There was no way for me to know what it might have been, just that it wasn't an animal. Besides, with all the hills and wide open space, it wouldn't surprise me if even a slight noise might travel for miles. And though it startled me, I wasn't about to let it disturb the tranquility of the night.

That was before a crash of metal on metal resounded through the air, causing me to bolt out of the chair. I made my way over to the rail between the peaks of the roof, trying to determine what it was or where it came from. It continued to echo across the fields as another boom, equally as loud, had me gripping the railing as I peered into the darkness. I scanned the area, barely able to make out the rolling hills beyond the fields, certain only that the large dense groupings of blackness had to be wooded sections. The house's outdoor lighting didn't extend far, leaving everything beyond in a grey, indeterminate hue.

As I turned away from the rail, another sound pierced the silence. The hollow, thudding noise stopped me in my tracks.

I don't know why, but goose bumps popped up all over my body, stripping me of the peace I'd felt moments ago—in its place was a strange apprehension. I turned back to the fields, uneasy about what I might see.

A tiny pinpoint of light appeared, seeming to bounce somewhere between earth and sky. The larger it grew, the more disturbed I became.

I rushed to the deck door, flung it open, and darted through it in a flash, only stopping long enough to make certain it closed securely behind me. I took the steep, narrow stairs two at a time, unconcerned for my safety. My heart was thundering as I closed the door into my room, my brain refusing to accept what I'd just seen.

"Impossible." I repeated the word over and over again. But no matter how many times I said it, the facts remained the same.

My childhood nightmare had just become reality.

Chapter 9

I don't know how long I remained with my back pressed against the door that led to the deck. I'd practically jumped from the top of the stairs to the entrance of my room and slammed the door behind me. My heart beat a strange staccato in my chest, skipping, then adding beats as I struggled for breath and a logical explanation of what I'd seen. Fingers that were suddenly frozen worked at the door knob, seeking a lock that wasn't there. It's why I remained transfixed where I was, my eyes searching the room for something heavy enough to shove in front of the door to block it. I settled on an occasional chair on the other side of the room. The problem was having to leave my post to get it.

I chided myself over the unreasonable fear that possessed me. After all, I'd been on top of a roof without a light to reveal my presence. There was no way for whatever—whoever—to know I was there. The distance had been far too great. Besides, I couldn't even be sure *what* I'd seen. The only explanation was the nightmare. It had remained at the forefront of my brain, influencing my perception and skewing it from the moment I'd heard that noise.

Draw.

The word came unbidden into my mind.

Draw it.

This time I remembered something Hadley once told me a long time ago.

"If it's all you can think about, the only thing occupying your mind to the point of distraction, then maybe the solution is to draw or paint it. Get it out of your head, Kelsey, and onto a canvas."

After placing the occasional chair in front of the door to the deck and the desk chair beneath the doorknob at the entrance to my room, I was ready to take Hadley's suggestion seriously.

Once I'd retrieved the necessary drawing tools and sketchpad from my backpack, I crawled onto the bed and placed my back securely against the headboard. All it took was flipping open the pad for my hands and brain to take over. Conscious thought was unnecessary. The only thing that mattered was to get it out of my head…

~~~

It was just before seven when I awoke with a stiff neck and graphite covering my hands. I reached up to rub my eyes but thought better of it. The trick would be getting off the bed without spreading the mess.

Somehow, the sketchpad and pencils ended up on the floor. Probably a good thing. I picked up the pad and closed the cover, not wanting to look at what I'd drawn, determined to put the experience behind me. What I *did* want was a shower and some
~~~

breakfast. After having only a few mints and a doughnut since lunch yesterday, I was starved.

I put the chairs back where they belonged, then fulfilled my first desire and had a long, hot shower.

The moment I opened the door of my room, the sunlight-filled staircase lifted my spirits. I made a mental note to remind myself to pull back the drapes and open the blinds as soon as I returned. But right now it was time to find something to eat. I hoped it wouldn't be too late to get some breakfast.

"Good morning, Kelsey." Susan greeted me with a smile. "We'll be busy today, so I hope you've plenty to keep yourself occupied."

"Not a problem. Anything I can do to help?"

"No, dear, but thanks for being so sweet and offering. We've got our housekeeping crew coming in today. Fanny and I help them get everything squared away, so we're able to get the cleaning completed in one day. Well, one day twice a week," she sighed. "It's a lot of work but worth it. Now, there's juice in the refrigerator and freshly baked croissants on the counter. Just help yourself."

"Sounds wonderful, thank you. Are you sure—"

"Oh, good, there are the girls. Gotta run, dear," she said in response to the sound of women's voices coming from the hallway. "There are sandwich fixings in the refrigerator for your lunch. You have a good day now." And she was gone.

There were several glasses on the counter as well as plates with silverware wrapped in napkins and placed in the middle of each plate. A note atop the place settings said to help myself. It was all the encouragement I needed. I chose the largest croissant in the batch, placed it on a plate that was fancier than anything I'd ever had—or would want, and poured myself a glass of orange juice. Closing the fridge, I spied an ornate decanter of honey and decided to drizzle a little on the croissant. I was prepared to take my breakfast to the table when a shaft of sunlight caught my attention. I followed it past the dining alcove to where French doors led out onto the patio.

The heady scent of cherry blossoms, flowering crabapple, and dogwood trees greeted me. Along with bushes of all kinds, from those with flowers, like lilacs and budding rosebushes, to boxwoods and different types of evergreens, the garden was burgeoning with life and seemed to go on forever. And the flowers! There was a rainbow of color represented from the typical spring flowers of tulips, daffodils, crocuses, and hyacinths intermixed with irises, dainty pansies, and I didn't know what all. There was very little grass. Instead, phlox and vinca appeared to blanket the entire area.

I sat at a table that was near a large, screened-in outdoor kitchen. There were several heavy wooden tables with cushioned chairs close by, ready for whatever outdoor event the Gradys decided to throw. I munched on a bite of croissant, amazed at the scene before me. Benches, statuary, and a couple gazebos dotted the landscape. A butterfly flitted past on its way to one of the many flowers. The joyful chirping of birds filled the air, chasing away what remained of the scare I'd had. I was about to take another bite when a "Good morning" sounded from out in the garden.

I turned in the direction of a voice I didn't recognize. How I'd missed the tall, thin woman where she sat beneath a pergola, I didn't know. When she waved me over, I picked up my breakfast items and joined her.

"You've grown up, Kelsey Carol, quite beautifully, too. I always said you had good bone structure." She had an abundance of curly white hair and a wide, toothy smile.

Here it was again—someone I didn't know who appeared well-acquainted with me.

"Do sit down, child. Despite what you may have heard, I don't bite."

"You're Emma Grady." I sat across from her, staring into her pale blue eyes. "Sean's got your eyes."

"And he better give them back." She laughed at her little joke. "It's one of the few things he seems to have inherited from me. But he's a good boy—most of the time. Loves his grandma and that's important."

I nodded my agreement. "May I ask how you know me?"

There was a slight shift in her eyes, a flutter that was there and gone so quickly I'd have missed it had I not been looking directly at her.

"Pictures, of course. Sean always had photos of his visits with your family. He'd come back and share them, regaling me with his stories. He's a great storyteller, you know." She leaned back in her chair. "He was very fond of your parents, loved watching them work. He was devastated by their deaths."

This was all news to me. She must have realized that as well because she reached out to pat my hand where it rested on the little table between us.

"Memory's a funny thing, Kelsey. Sometimes our brains seem to just piecemeal information, filtering out sections that may or may not be important." She shook her head. "Perhaps it gets so filled with minutia it has trouble distinguishing the difference." She appeared to be studying me, waiting for a reaction. I didn't have one. Hadley often voiced something along the same lines.

Despite priding myself on my excellent recall, there *were* times when things seemed slightly out of reach. My aunt would say it was likely caused by stressing over a situation. And because she never appeared concerned about it, neither was I. Emma Grady's statement was confirmation of what Hadley had told me all along.

"I didn't remember that about Sean and my parents until you mentioned it just now." I asked whether she minded if I continued with my breakfast and was thrilled when she said I should go ahead.

"Fanny's an exceptional cook. And her baked goods are beyond compare. Her mother was good, but Fanny..." She grinned. "She took her mother's recipes, put her own touches on them, and excelled. I believe she'll really enjoy having that bed and breakfast the sisters are always talking about."

"So you support their dream?" I took another bite of croissant and tried not to smack my lips.

"A hundred percent. I'd not have encouraged all the work on the house if I didn't. Now," she leaned slightly forward, brushing away a fly that seemed to be overly interested in her hair. "What about you, Kelsey? Sean said you were painting again."

Oh he did, did he?

"I am. For now." Brilliant, Kelsey. You get so worked up over what that bully said to his grandmother that you can't put together anything better than a couple two-word sentences? Well, that wasn't going to happen.

"I ran into a bit of a problem with the curfew, but once it's over, I've several places I'd like to paint." I drank a little juice. "First, I want to finish St. Andrew's. I, uh, kinda got interrupted just as it was getting interesting and am anxious to get back to it."

"Sean said you liked to paint outside in the dark. However one finds inspiration it's best to follow that path. You'd understand that better than most, having had parents who were artists. I seem to remember your father preferring early mornings." She stopped abruptly, seeming to realize what she'd said.

"He did," I quickly answered, hoping to put her at ease. "As well as the moments just before dusk."

"Ah," she nodded, rising. When I started to get up, she shook her head. "Stay put, young lady, and eat your breakfast. I've been sitting too long and need to stretch my legs."

"Mrs. Grady—"

"Emma."

"Emma," I grinned. "May I ask you a question before you go?" If she was ultimately in charge of the house renovation, maybe she was the one I needed to ask about using the roof of the garage.

"Never be afraid of asking, Kelsey. After all, the worst case scenario is a refusal of your request."

"True. But when you're staying in someone's home, you also don't want to appear too forward."

"Touché. And the question?"

"I wondered if I could use the roof of the garage to paint. It's got the perfect view of the house and-"

"Done. I'll make arrangements with Sean to provide you access. He'd mentioned you might want it, so he's already prepared to grant your wish." She chuckled. "That surprises you, doesn't it? Oh, I know all about the little tiffs the two of you used to have. But he always supported your talent—even when you stopped believing in yourself." Her enigmatic statement and smile caught me off guard and she knew it. "I'll be seeing you again soon, Miss Kelsey."

Chapter 10

The innuendo from various people I'd met since coming to Seaton was driving me nuts. Statements about how I should remember them, how they knew me, what was up with that? How could I have such a hole in my memory? And I wasn't buying what Hadley and Emma said about my brain being too full, etcetera. One or two instances, maybe. Not what I was experiencing. There *had* to be a better explanation.

And I knew the one person capable of answering all my questions.

After I'd taken care of my breakfast dishes, I returned to the garden, settling into a pretty little gazebo near the brook that ran through the back side of the property. The narrow creek danced over rocks, wending its way toward a stand of trees nearby. The little footbridge Susan had mentioned appeared to spill out onto a pathway that led into the grove. Like everything else about the Grady's home, the garden was picturesque and beautiful.

The air was still, and except for the sounds of nature, quiet. The peaceful setting and privacy seemed a perfect place to call my aunt. When her voicemail picked up, I left a message, asking her to give me a call back when she had the time to spend on the phone.

"We need to talk, Aunt Hadley—it's not an emergency, but it is important. And I'm pretty sure you already have an idea what it's about." I pocketed my cell, pulled my legs onto the bench, and leaned back to enjoy my surroundings. The gentle babbling of the brook and birdsong soon lulled me to sleep—though I wouldn't have realized I'd nodded off had I not been awakened by a scuffling sound as someone passed by.

"Sean?" I tried to stand only to discover that my legs had also fallen asleep—painfully so.

"I didn't see you there." He'd stopped but didn't look happy about it. "Are you ok? You look kinda funny."

"Legs fell asleep. Hey, I wanted to thank you for getting my computer set up."

"I told you I would." The snarky retort reminded me of the old Sean. The one I'd hoped had disappeared with age. "That all?"

"Yeah, I mean, I just thought maybe—" It was no longer my legs making me feel off balance. The man before me wasn't anything like the guy I'd spoken with the day before. Or was he?

"Get over yourself, Kelsey. I'm here to see my grandmother." He continued on his way without another word.

Get over myself? What was that supposed to mean? Did he think I was asking him out or something? Because that wasn't my intention. Furthest thing from my mind. All I'd been trying to do was have a conversation, bring up what Emma had said about him and my parents. Get over myself?! What arrogance!

I was saved from further introspection when my phone rang. Expecting it to be Hadley returning my call, I prepared myself for a difficult conversation.

"Are you all right?" A deep male voice brought me up short.

What was this? Of course I was all right.

"Detec-er-Adam. Everything's fine. Is there something I can do for you?" Not a very smooth way to switch gears.

"Did I catch you at a bad time?"

Bad time? "No, no. I was just expecting a call from my aunt." I hoped he didn't expect me to confide in him as he'd suggested I could do yesterday.

"I'll only keep you a moment." He cleared his throat. "I wondered if you might like to go to dinner with me tomorrow evening. We've an excellent barbeque restaurant, if you're interested."

I accepted his invitation, and after a short discussion, he agreed to meeting at the restaurant at seven. It would give me plenty of time to pick up the key from Director Hanson and allow me the chance to set up my equipment on the roof of the Historical Society. As I'd said earlier to Emma, I was anxious to get back to my painting of St. Andrew's. Adam didn't seem particularly pleased about that aspect of the night but also didn't chide me. Perhaps he realized bossing me around wasn't good etiquette when asking me on a date.

I admit to being flattered. Then there was the issue of his being a source of information. Besides, he seemed like a nice guy and wasn't bad to look at.

An abundance of pent up energy made me feel ready to jump out of my skin. The solution was to walk it off.

Since I was curious about the path through the woods and where it went, it seemed a logical choice. So, after stopping for a moment on the footbridge and watching as the brook skipped over the rocks, chattering happily on its way through the property, I crossed over into the trees.

I followed the well-worn gravel path as it wended its way between the trees, emptying out into a clearing that contained a large greenhouse. There didn't appear to be anyone around, and since the building wasn't locked, I didn't have any qualms about going inside.

It was warmer and a lot more humid in the greenhouse than it was outside. You could smell the soil, fertilizer, and the various scents of different plants and flowers. Other than the hum of equipment to circulate the air, it was quiet. I strode through rows of vegetables—lettuce, tomatoes, peppers and onions among other things—amazed by the variety. I wasn't very far into the building, about to enter an aisle filled with flowers, when I heard the angry voice.

"It was a harebrained idea to allow her to come here. This is insane. You try to protect your secrets, and then—" Fanny came into view at the far end of the greenhouse. Though she appeared to be talking to herself, it was obvious from the glint of silver in her ear that she was on a headset. I flushed with embarrassment when her eyes raised and met mine.

"Kelsey, you're here." She pulled the headset from her ear and stuffed it into the apron she wore. "Come to check out our greenhouse? It's really quite something. Emma started it years ago. It supplies us with fruits, vegetables, and berries all year long, as well as flowers for every season. I would've been glad to bring you out here if I'd known you were interested."

All I could do was nod, wondering what I was supposed to do now. We both knew she'd been referring to me, but she was covering it up better than I was. I got the feeling she'd had a lot more practice at that sort of thing.

"Hi, Fanny. I hope I'm not disturbing you. Um, Susan said you guys would be busy today, so I decided to explore. I hope you don't mind."

"Not at all. It's a natural extension of things once you cross the footbridge. I always thought Emma chose the perfect setting for the greenhouse in the middle of the clearing."

She was now within arm's length of me. Though my face still burned, there was no hint of discomfort on hers.

"Yeah, this is great. So, I'll bet the veggies for our salad came from right here."

She nodded, a little twinkle in her eyes. "Not only are our vegetables better than any you can get in a store, but gathering them gives me the opportunity to come out here and tinker. I've always loved digging in the dirt and watching things grow. Besides," she winked. "It gives me a little alone time. Susan hates it here, and Emma rarely comes anymore, so it's just me and the plants." She wound her arm through mine, and a chill went up my spine. "Let me take you on a tour."

Chapter 11

It was apparent someone had been in my room. The drapes had been pushed back and the blinds opened. Even though I'd made the bed, it was clear it had been remade with clean sheets. And there were fresh towels in the bathroom. Though it shouldn't have surprised me, it did. I supposed when the cleaning crew got started it was only natural for them to include my room since it, too, was occupied.

Sunlight filled the room, making it far more inviting than it had been when I'd left hours earlier. If anyone noticed the slight rearrangement of furniture, they obviously hadn't cared. The occasional chair was exactly where I put it, a short distance from the door to the roof.

Walking across the recently vacuumed carpet made me feel guilty for having traipsed through the house with my shoes on. I slipped out of my sandals and made a mental note to remember this was the Gradys' home, not a hotel.

The window seat called to me, and I answered by sitting down, tucking a throw pillow in the small of my back, and drawing my legs onto the bench. Gazing out the window overlooking the vast fields and rolling hills, I marveled at how innocuous and non-threatening the scenery was now, in contrast to what I'd witnessed early that morning. Had I really seen something, or had the odd sounds dredged up my old nightmares, causing a kind of hallucination?

My sketchbook. I scanned the room twice before discovering it and the drawing pencils on the desk near my laptop. I knew I'd left them on the nightstand. Maybe the housekeepers thought the desk was a more appropriate place for them. There was brief consideration of getting up to take a look at what I'd drawn, but I was too comfortable to move. Instead, I grabbed another of the throw pillows and hugged it to my chest as I stretched out onto the window seat.

One of the things I hate most about cell phones is how they always seem to ring at the wrong time. Yes, I was waiting for a call from my aunt, but why did it have to come at the precise moment when I was so incredibly relaxed I could have fallen asleep. Thinking about the last time I'd dozed off this morning and the unpleasant encounter with Sean, I didn't have high expectations for this call to go any better than that face to face.

"I don't suppose you'll let it go and come back home?" There was a note of resignation in Hadley's voice. I hated to upset her but felt it was necessary if I was ever going to get some answers.

"What don't I know?" Though I tried to keep it from sounding like an accusation, I knew I was unsuccessful.

"That's not an easy question to answer, Kelsey, especially on the phone. If you'd just come home-"

"That's not an answer, Aunt Hadley. It's a request that, frankly, I'm refusing outright. I'm sorry if this upsets you, but can you imagine how unsettling it is to feel like the only person in the world who doesn't know what's going on—and it's all about me. What happened to me, Hadley?"

I heard her intake of breath, the ragged way it sounded when she released it, but I refused to be swayed. "This is the first time in years that I've been able to really tap into my muse." I continued, trying to sway her. "I've got the feeling it won't continue if I leave now."

"This isn't easy for me, either. Not the memories and definitely not you being in Seaton. You know I was against it from the start."

"And you know I need to make my own way. But this isn't about me cutting the apron strings; it's about people saying I should remember them, people acting like they know me when I have absolutely no idea who they are and what they're talking about. Emma Grady gave me the same kind of explanation for my lack of memory as you have over the years. I trusted you, still trust you. If there's a problem, if there's something wrong with me, you need to tell me, *please*."

Silence on the other end of the line had me wondering if our call had been disconnected. Just as I was about to hang up and call her back, she spoke.

"Do you remember that old TV program you used to love, the one where the character, Sam, jumped into other people's lives to try to change the past for the better?"

"*Quantum Leap*. What has that got to do-"

"You really loved that show. I never believed it was a coincidence that you were so enamored by a program where the lead character's memory was described in much the same way the doctors described yours."

"Like Swiss cheese, full of holes that only sometimes get filled in?"

"Honey, you were so traumatized by your parents' murders that you were like a robot. You would follow instructions, but," she sighed. "The best way to put it is that you really weren't there. In time, the nightmares passed, and you were more yourself. We thought it best to let you recover in your own time. After a while, the therapist deemed you whole again."

"Maybe on the outside, but I've always had questions, wanted to know the truth of what happened and make sure the guilty parties were brought to justice."

"I want that too, Kels. We all do. But there's a saying your grandfather had when I was little that I think applies here. He would chide your mother and me about not poking the bear. Do you understand? You need to, because that's exactly what you're doing. And I'm afraid if you keep on poking, that none of us are going to like the outcome." Hadley's voice shook, and I could tell she was crying. It broke my heart to have upset her, and I tried my best to reassure her. It was quickly evident that no matter what I said, she wouldn't be assuaged.

"I'm a lot stronger than you or I know. God's on our side, and He'll never let us down."

"You keep praying," she said firmly. "And

never forget the evil that's out there. I love you, Kelsey, and wish you'd come back home. Either way, I'm here for you."

When we finally hung up, my heart ached from worrying about my aunt. Despite all that was said, I'd come away without the answers I'd sought. If getting them meant poking grandpa's bear, I was ready to do it. And I would start by being brave enough to look at the sketch I'd done this morning. I went straight to the desk and flipped open the sketchpad, bypassing the few drawings I'd done of different buildings in Seaton. It should have been on the sixth page, but the only thing there was a strange group of smudges across the paper.

"What the devil?"

I flipped through each page, making sure none of them had stuck together. The sketch wasn't here. That's when I noticed the small fragments of tattered paper where the page had been torn out.

Someone had taken my sketch.

Chapter 12

I was looking under the bed when I realized the futility of my search. Housekeeping had been in earlier and cleaned, and unlike some places I'd stayed in the past, it was doubtful they wouldn't have vacuumed under the bed. Even if I'd accidentally thrown away the sketch, the trash had been emptied. Bottom line: whatever I'd drawn was gone.

My thoughts were scrambled, tumbling over one another much like the balls in a bingo cage. I'd thought I was safe, secure and confident in myself and my life for the first time since I was twelve. What did it mean? Having a Swiss cheese memory for a fictional character worked. Having one in reality, not so much. It was awkward, made me self-conscious, and downright uncomfortable. Good investigator I was! How could I help expose the perpetrators of my parents' murders when I didn't really know myself?

This was ridiculous! Just because there were a few bumps in my memory didn't mean I wasn't a strong, capable individual. Motivation was something I had in abundance, and if anyone thought they could derail me by swiping a sketch or bringing up part of the past I didn't recall, they had another think coming. I'm a survivor, and if anyone messed with me, I'd show them exactly what I was made of!

~~~

Even when you're on vacation, there are mundane things you need to do. Laundry is one of them.

I'd managed to slip out of the house with my bag of dirty clothes without anyone noticing. While I was sure the sisters wouldn't have minded me using their washer and dryer, getting out and away from everyone and everything was what I wanted.

Between wash loads, I sketched some children who'd found a way to quietly amuse themselves in the confines of the laundromat. They noticed what I was doing and were thrilled when I gave them the pictures I'd drawn of them. Their mother offered to pay me and couldn't believe when I said it wasn't necessary—her appreciation of the drawing was enough.

By the time the last load was in the dryer, only one other person remained in the laundromat. The drone of the machines and repeat of *Jeopardy!* on TV was a perfect backdrop for letting my imagination run free. I filled several pages with sketches of flowers and birds as well as fanciful depictions of anything that came to mind. A perfect time for my cell to signal I had an email message.

"Will contact you soon. S. Pattison"

The email address looked bogus, of course. That
~~~

would've been too easy.

"But I've got your attention now, bud," I muttered, giving the area a quick glance. The lady was emptying out a dryer, totally unaware of my existence—or so it seemed.

My dryer buzzed, and soon I was back on the road to the Gradys' grand home. It would be a quiet night, a little TV after a light supper and then to bed. I had a date with Adam Davies tomorrow evening followed by painting by moonlight. What could be better than that?

Chapter 13

As I rounded the arc to the garage, I heard the tinny sound of a small horn behind me. A look in the rearview mirror revealed Emma at the wheel of a golf cart. The moment I parked in front of the garage, she pulled in next to me.

"Take a ride with me, Kelsey?" Though formed as a question, I had the feeling it was more than a simple request—she didn't want me to refuse. She seemed in a bit of a hurry, and the way she kept glancing around made me feel she didn't want to be seen out and about. Just another in a long list of things I didn't understand about the interactions of this family.

I'd barely gotten situated in the cart when she was off on whatever mission or adventure she had in mind.

"I believe that belongs to you." Emma nodded to a raggedy piece of paper that lay between us. I immediately recognized it as the sheet that had been torn out of my sketchbook. It had been ripped and crumpled at one time, then carefully flattened and taped back together.

"How?" I picked up the page as it lay, the blank side up, still not ready to look at what I'd drawn.

"It may sound odd, but I frequently check through the trash before it's collected by our garbage men. I've found it to be helpful, even enlightening at times. It's also explained some of the, well, let's call them misplaced items that have gone missing from time to time." Emma turned onto a gravel road that led into a grove of trees and then out onto one of the many rolling hills. "I thought we might need some privacy." She said, answering my unspoken question. "Fanny and Susan are still busy with the cleaning women, but that doesn't mean they're not keeping an eye on other things as well."

"I saw Fanny at the greenhouse today. It was unlocked..."

"Surprised her, huh?" Emma chuckled. "That girl's never liked surprises. Complete opposite of her sister."

"I don't think she wants me here." I decided not to elaborate. Since I'd no idea who I could really trust, it was best to leave it at speculation on my part.

"Don't be silly, Kelsey. Fanny loves company. She's just a mite more reserved than her sister, that's all."

I gazed back at the paper in my lap. "Why would anyone take this? Or the "things" you've mentioned? Do you know who the culprit is?"

"Culprit," now she really laughed. "I like that. And, no, I don't. Have my suspicions but without proof, it would only cause more trouble. Things aren't always cut and dried or as they might appear." She stopped the cart on a hill above what appeared to be the remains of a house—probably the area Susan warned me about.

"This is as close as I care to get to the old place. If you ask me, it's haunted. Either way, it always gave me the willies. Luke knew how I felt and never even suggested we move in here after we were married. The new house was still under construction, so Luke altered the design to include our own little apartment. Moved in before it was completed and have been there ever since." She switched off the cart before turning to me.

"By the time Luke and I were married, it was common knowledge how the family made their money during the depression. Bootlegging. Prohibition destroyed a lot of people and communities, but not Seaton. It not only survived but thrived under the watchful eyes of the Gradys. They made sure there were enough legitimate ventures to cover what they were doing, and there wasn't a man in town that would've turned them in."

"Fascinating. But all that ended with the repeal of Prohibition. Right?"

She shrugged. "I liked to believe that Luke and his father were totally on the up and up. That they weren't tempted to indulge in more illegal activities. Besides, Luke was a good man, for the most part. Still, there were rumors of other nefarious ventures. No matter what I believed, my parents weren't as trusting. My folks insisted I keep my eyes and ears open to make certain there were no shenanigans going on." She chuckled. "So, I guess you could say my habit of checking through the trash came about honestly—all in an effort to reassure my family that their baby girl was safe and not in the middle of a gang of thugs."

"And?"

Her pale blue eyes swept over the remains of the original Grady homestead. "Cabe would've finished the demolition in spite of his brother's protests but... Then he was gone. He was always such a good, sweet boy." She brushed a tear from her cheek. "I'd feel a lot better if they just came out here with some heavy equipment and destroyed the rest of this eyesore. It's the old root cellar where they kept the liquor. There's just something about it that makes my skin crawl. And after having a look at your drawing, I'm pretty sure it bothers you as well."

"I've never been here, but I'd be able to see it from the rooftop deck—in daylight."

"You would. And I'm pretty sure you saw it at night as well." Emma reached out and touched my hand where it lay between us on the seat. "Why don't you flip it over, Kelsey. See what it is that someone didn't want you to have."

"It was the noise that got my attention," I explained, looking in the direction of the house. Though it was some distance away, it was clearly visible, even the deck was easy to make out. Specific details weren't clear, but that wasn't a surprise.

"What did you see, Kelsey?" Emma prodded gently.

I shook my head. "It was so wonderfully quiet, and then there were these loud bangs that seemed to echo forever. I got up to check it out, to try to discover where it was coming from. Then I saw these lights..."

Emma didn't wait for further explanation; she reached over and flipped the sketch. "Is this what you saw, Kelsey? Did you see that early this morning?"

"This morning?" The timeframe seemed off somehow—just like the drawing. I'd seen lights that appeared to defy gravity, maybe a shadow or two, but this sketch, this sketch was straight out of my old nightmares. Strange lights and wavy images that may or may not be human, one of which was running in my direction. His hands ended in claws that dripped teardrop shaped liquid. Blood.

"It's...not...possible." My hands shook as I shredded the paper Emma Grady had taken such care in putting back together. "It's not real. Not what I saw. I—I don't know what I saw, but it wasn't that."

She took me into her arms to soothe me. "It's all right, Kelsey. We all have nightmares. And if anything's going to give them to you, it's that place right over there. Like I said, haunted. Don't you worry now. We're going back to the house and have a nice supper. Talk about pleasant things. How's that sound."

Exactly like the evening I'd wanted after my drive from town. I wondered if it were possible now?

I was told something once a long time ago, something about my parents' investigation.

As Emma drove us back to the house, I dug in my Swiss cheese brain trying to remember. By the time she'd pulled up next to my car, I had it.

Every clue brings more questions than answers.
I believed it was a good analogy of life.

Chapter 14

Though I'd really wanted to spend the rest of the evening alone, it didn't turn out that way. Emma had been serious about our having a "nice supper" when we got back to the house. What neither of us counted on was that Susan and Fanny would be joining us.

Since the weather was still warm, the sisters set out the meal on the screened-in patio. The luscious smell of chicken frying on the grill filled the air. Along with Fanny's "special" potato salad and baked beans, Susan had made a strawberry pie for dessert—with berries from their own greenhouse, of course. Afterward, we all assisted in getting everything into the kitchen and the dishwasher.

Even after a day of cleaning the massive house, the sisters were in high spirits. I noticed Fanny watching me a bit surreptitiously and wondered if she was still miffed at my startling her in the greenhouse. Susan, on the other hand, was even more talkative than usual, insisting we play at least one game of Crazy Eights.

"My favorite!" Emma declared with a clap. "Do stay for a game, Kelsey. It'll be fun."

Susan winked at me. "It helps Emma relax,

doesn't it, dear?"

"It does, indeed. I think after the day we've each had it will be good for all of us. Especially for you, Fanny. You do look especially tired tonight." Emma reached out and touched Fanny's elbow. The look the two exchanged was one of genuine affection for each other. Something I hadn't seen between Emma and Susan.

The one game turned to three as the ladies reveled at besting one another. I had to admit that joining them was more fun than I'd had in a while. I enjoyed their company and knew it was better than mulling over the events of the last few days. It also provided a little more insight into their family dynamics. As I'd noted earlier, Fanny and Emma appeared to have a special relationship, while Susan gave me the impression she was playacting.

By the end of the third raucous game, Emma declared she'd had enough. She and Fanny excused themselves, and when I stood to do the same, Susan rose and tucked her arm in mine. She walked me up to my room, chattering on about the future of the house. I didn't think she realized she'd mentioned most of it before.

"Oh, I saw Sean today. He wasn't in a very good mood, so I didn't think it was the best time to bring up using the garage roof for your painting. I did tell you, didn't I, that it's pretty much his domain—the apartment, you know. Why, he won't let *anyone* step foot in the space, not even housekeeping. Very particular about it all. He calls it his writing studio." She stopped for a breath. "You have to go through the apartment to get onto the roof. He's made a nice little deck there, very private, away from the rest of us."

The more she talked, the more confused I became. Emma had said Sean already knew I'd want to paint the main house from the garage. She'd told me that all he needed was a head's up when I was ready.

Of course the conversation with Emma was before my encounter with Sean in the garden. He hadn't wanted anything to do with me then. What had changed?

"Don't worry, dear, I'll get him to cooperate. You just have to be patient."

She'd said that before, too.

"So, how do you like your room? Is it as comfortable as the inn?"

"Far better." I assured her. "You were right about the bed. It's nicer than what I have at home." By now we were at the door to my room. Though I was ready for some alone time, Susan didn't appear to be.

"I'm so pleased. Means we're on the right track." She gave me a quick hug. "Thanks for being such a good sport and playing cards with us. Emma was having a good day and I knew it would help her settle down for the night. Might not seem that way with how she was carrying on, but it will. All the activity seems to improve her mood for a few days, which is good for all of us. She can be difficult and cause a lot of problems, but she can also be a sweetheart. I prefer the sweetheart."

Since I didn't really know Emma, I had to take her word for it, even if it was the complete opposite of the Emma I'd spent time with today. I needed to face it, no one seemed to be who I thought they were—not even Susan, who I'd known most of my life.

I opened the door to my room, hoping it would signal my intentions. It didn't work: Susan continued to chat, bouncing from one subject to another.

"I'm planning a trip to Columbia tomorrow and wondered if you might like to come along. We could do a spa day, get a mani-pedi, shop, really get to know one another. If you don't have any plans, I'd love your company."

Her enthusiasm made my answer difficult. "Thanks for the offer, but I have to decline. I've a date tomorrow even-"

"A date? How interesting! I hope you don't mind my asking who it's with."

"Not at all. It's Detective Adam Davies."

She almost jumped in excitement, not seeming at all upset by the rejection. "He's such a fine young man. Very dedicated to his job and the community."

"I'm looking forward to it." I entered my room. Susan followed, asking where Adam was taking me. I told her and hoped that would be enough to satisfy her to let me go. That's when I realized it might be a good idea to let her know that I'd be out till early morning, painting from the roof of the Historical Society.

"Duly noted. But really, Kelsey, is it necessary for you to work at night? Bad things happen in the dark. And yes, I know bad things happen at all times of the day and night, it's just..." She shook her head and sighed. "There are more people around in the daytime. More eyes on you."

"True. It's also one of the reasons I prefer painting at night. I like being alone, helps me get in the groove. And you don't need to worry about me." I told her how adept I was at protecting myself with my easel and some common self-defense moves. It seemed to reassure her.

"You know, Hadley never liked this fixation of yours. It's just not normal, Kelsey. But I suppose you know what's best for you." She gave me a weak smile before bidding me goodnight.

After she'd gone, I sat on the edge of the bed, running the events of the day through my mind. The highlight was S. Pattison's email. Trying to sort through the rest, how the sketch had been ripped from my book and retrieved by Emma—coming to grips with the sketch itself. That was difficult. But Hadley's revelation about my Swiss cheese memory was the clincher.

I was tired and confused, yes, but was sure it all tied together. Somewhere deep inside my brain there were answers to piece everything into a cohesive picture.

And if I could put this puzzle together, maybe I could figure out a way to solve my parents' murders.

There was a lock on the past, and I was positive that somehow I was the key.

Chapter 15

"I'm sorry, Miss Carol, but we can't seem to locate the key. Are you sure you brought it back?" Once more I explained to the administrative assistant that the police had taken the key when they took me to the station.

"Director Hanson knows all about it. Is there any way I can speak with him?"

"I'm sorry; he's out of the office right now. I'll be happy to leave him a message."

I repeated my request to use the roof that evening, even offered to pay for a locksmith to make a new key. The woman assured me Hanson would give me a call back at his earliest convenience. I hoped it would be sooner rather than later.

Still, in preparation of things going my way, I gathered my stuff together, checking each bag to make certain everything was in the right place. I would operate under the assumption that Hanson would approve my request. If he didn't...

~~~
~~~

It had been a tough sell, but the director finally agreed to allow me one more night on his roof. When I offered to pay for a new key, he informed me that wouldn't be necessary because an officer had returned the one confiscated a short time before. I thanked him profusely and agreed to meet him at four to get the key and to sign another "contract" for use of the space. He was much shorter with me than he'd been before, but I couldn't blame him. I'm sure he didn't like having been contacted by the cops a few nights before anymore than I'd liked being hauled in by them.

I didn't understand the building design, why the steps to the roof were encased in the way they were, outside the main structure, accessed only by a door from the street and the second story of the Historical Society. The design might be weird, but if it hadn't been, I'd never have been given access to the roof in the first place.

Armed with the key, I returned to my car to begin the arduous task of unloading my equipment. I slipped on a backpack and drew out two canvas bags for the first trip up the narrow, dimly lit staircase. If I continued to paint like this, I'd need to get a couple of rolling cases to store my things so it would be easier to move from place to place.

"Need a hand?" I immediately recognized Adam Davies's deep voice.

"Hi!" I turned to greet him with a smile. "Yes, your help would be awesome. The stairs are steep and so narrow it's next to impossible to carry everything at once—even if I could."

"Are you sure this stuff isn't multiplying when

you're not looking?" He chuckled. "Now I understand why it took two officers to bring it all in."

"That's because they were dragging me along with them. If they'd allowed me to help..."

He drew the bag containing my easel over his shoulder. "For all intents and purposes you were being detained for breaking curfew. You're lucky they didn't put you in cuffs." His cell rang, and he moved a short distance away to answer it.

"Best laid plans," he said, placing the easel case back into the trunk. "I've got to go. If you want to leave this till later, I'll be happy to help you get set up."

Happy? I didn't think he approved of my process.

He walked me to the door, took the key to unlock it, then held it for me to go through.

"Keep this safe," he said returning the key. "And make sure the door closes securely behind you." He told me he'd see me later then hurried off.

When I got back to my car, I found Sean leaning up against it. His arms were crossed, and he had a smug grin plastered on his face.

"Took you long enough."

"If you're here to irritate me, you've succeeded. So, you can go now." I proceeded to my trunk, trying hard to ignore him.

"You're on your game." He laughed. "That's a good one. I'm just trying to figure out what makes you think my intention is anything but honorable."

"Maybe because I'm still trying to get over myself." I quipped.

"Oh, yeah. Sorry about that." He began unloading the rest of my stuff. "I was a little... preoccupied when I saw you yesterday. Bad time at work, that kind of thing."

Unlike Adam, he didn't offer to unlock the door or hold it for me to go through first. He did make sure I got inside before it closed on me. For Sean, that was as much of a gentleman as I'd expect.

Once on the roof, he was actually very helpful, asking where I wanted to set up, assisting in arranging things at my direction. It surprised, even pleased, me how interested and encouraging he seemed. I just hoped my reactions didn't show.

"This really is a great spot to paint the church," he remarked. He leaned slightly forward over the waist-high wall edging the roof. "Hope you're not afraid of heights."

"It is, and I'm not concerned." I finished placing the mosquito netting over the easel and stool, readying it for tonight. Although the forecast didn't call for rain, I decided not to risk the canvas so I left it in its waterproof case.

"So, now what? You wait up here till dark?" He looked around. "Doesn't look like a fun place to spend several hours."

Was he fishing because it seemed like he was?

"I've got plans." I motioned to him that it was time to go.

"Plans, huh? Sounds mysterious, Kelsey. And here I was about to ask you to have dinner with me. I thought it would give us a chance to catch up." He followed me off the roof onto the landing of the staircase.

Even though I knew the door locked automatically, I made a big show of testing the knob before heading down the stairs.

"I thought we'd already done that. You remember the other day when I caught you ogling my car."

"Not ogling. Admiring. I've fond—"

"Memories. So you said."

"Now who's not playing nice?"

I didn't have to look at him to know he was smirking, that the right corner of his lip would be curled slightly and there'd be crinkles surrounding his incredibly pale blue eyes.

Where did that come from?

I guess the memories he mentioned brought back some of my own.

Out on the sidewalk, I thanked him for his assistance, and to my astonishment, he took a bow.

"Always ready to help a lady." He said without a grain of sarcasm.

He turned and strode off down the street before I had a chance to reply. I never did come up with a retort.

Chapter 16

The restaurant was a little loud but smelled so good the noise was worth it. Despite being busy, we were seated without having to wait in line—I wondered if it was Adam's reputation or if he'd called ahead. Maybe a bit of both.

"They have the best barbeque this side of Kansas City," he told me as we were escorted to a booth by a hostess dressed like a cowgirl. He made sure I was comfortable before he sat down. "And they don't believe in having a TV in every corner. There's one in the bar, that's it. They take pride in their food and believe the customers provide the atmosphere."

"That's unusual these days. About the TVs, not the food." Brilliant as always. "Wow! The menu's a bit overwhelming."

"Maybe it'd be best to order a sampler platter for two—we choose four meats and two sides. And trust me when I say we'll be taking home doggie bags."

"Howdy, pardner!" Our waitress sort of sashayed up to our table. "Why, Detective, it's nice to see ya'll again. Ma'am." She winked at him and gave me a nod. "What can I get ya'll tonight?"

"Hi, Sheila. How's your dad? That was a nasty fall he took the other day."

"He's better." She grinned. "Thanks for asking, Adam. Any way you could convince him to retire or at least take a desk job? Running after a suspect isn't as easy as it used to be."

"He was picking up curfew violators," he explained to me. And to her, "Sarge isn't about to listen to my advice. Better coming from you and your brother."

She took our drink orders—an iced tea for me, a beer for him—then left us to decide what to include on our platter. It didn't take long to agree on pulled pork, chopped beef brisket, shredded chicken, and barbeque wings along with steak fries and coleslaw. It sounded good but messy.

"I'm sorry about her dad." I said, stacking and restacking the menus, more than a little embarrassed.

"He's a good man, and it shouldn't have happened. I'm just glad you're not the reason. So, stop feeling guilty. Ok?" He took the menus and set them at the edge of the table.

"Now, Kelsey Carol, have you always wanted to be an artist?" He sat back and smiled.

I stared deeply into his eyes, trying to gauge what sort of question this might be and realized it was an attempt to put me at ease. It could be a trick of a trained investigator, but the more I watched him, the more I trusted this was only the kind of chitchat you had on a date.

"I think so. My parents always said I knew how to draw before I could walk. How about you? You always want to be a cop?"

Sheila set our drinks in front of us, apologizing—to Adam—that it took so long to get back to us. After she'd taken our order, Adam leaned in, motioning for me to do the same.

"She's had a bit of a crush on me for years," he explained. "Guess it's all the time I spent with her dad. Anyway, in answer to your question, yes, being in law enforcement's always been my first love."

"And where does the history buff come in?" His eyebrows rose. In surprise? I couldn't be sure. "You said something about helping my parents. I also saw it on the city's website."

"History is a different sort of passion. I believe that knowing the past, where one comes from, should be important to all of us. It puts things in perspective, shows us where we've been and where we're going."

I nodded my agreement. "And what do you do in your spare time? Any hobbies?"

"What spare time?" He laughed. "When I'm not being a police officer, I volunteer at the fire station. Whatever down time I have, I read—mostly history books, but I do like to throw in an occasional thriller."

"Ah. Makes sense. I used to read a lot of mysteries."

"Not romance?" The glint in his eyes told me he was trying to get a rise out of me.

"Occasionally." I leaned forward, putting my arms on the table. "Now I prefer watching cold cases on TV." I'd meant it as a joke, tit-for-tat for his comment about romances. He didn't take it that way. His total demeanor changed.

"I wouldn't think that would be a good way for you to spend your time." His tone was clipped. Detective Adam Davies gave me a piercing glare. His back stiffened, and the smile vanished.

Silence ensued, making the wait for our dinner uncomfortable. I refused to be intimidated by the glare, or by the blatant way he flirted with the waitress when she returned with our food. Although the barbeque was good, I picked at my meal. I hadn't planned on eating much, anyway. Now, I barely ate at all.

There was no real conversation, only polite exchanges that were stiff and awkward. He was still eating when I excused myself and escaped to the restroom. I wiped my face and arms with a paper towel drenched in cold water, trying to get up the courage to return to the booth and the equally cold stare of the detective.

I left the restroom, buoyed by the fact the date couldn't last much longer. I hadn't gone far when someone grabbed my elbow, pulling me back into the shadows of the hallway.

"Hey!" I wrenched my arm from Sean Grady's grasp. "What do you think you're doing?"

He leaned in so close I could smell beer on his breath.

"If I were you, I'd be more careful about the company I kept." He growled.

Chapter 17

My head reeled from Sean's behavior and nasty tone. I guess he was more like his mother than I'd believed. The way he flip-flopped from "good Sean" to "bad Sean" was as odd as Susan's hot and cold attitudes and repetitious stories about the house—and a lot like the Sean Grady I'd seen described on the internet. It didn't help that I'd just spent over an hour in the company of a man who clearly wanted to be any place but with me. It wasn't the worst date I'd been on, but it was close.

Adam was ready to leave when I got back. He jumped up so quickly I thought he might stumble on the slightly raised platform our booth sat on. He didn't, thank God. He took hold of the same arm Sean had grabbed, gripping it so hard I was sure it would leave a nasty bruise.

He walked me to my car in silence, broken only when I thanked him for dinner and said I'd had a nice time.

"You don't need to lie, Kelsey. I overreacted and apologize for ruining the night."

"And I shouldn't have said what I did. I only meant it as a joke, not a slight against you or the depar-"

He put a finger against my lips. "I know. Let's leave it at that."

I nodded, glad we'd cleared the air while hoping he wouldn't try to kiss me.

"I'll follow you back to the Historical Society. I want to make certain you're safe before I leave."

He not only followed me back, he got out of his car and stayed by my side until I'd gotten inside the stairwell. After the door closed, I heard him try the knob to make sure it had locked.

"Happy painting," came his muffled voice.

I remained at the door until I heard a car drive away.

~~~

It was a lot chillier on the roof than I'd expected. I'd prepared for such a contingency—a sweater and overalls that took the place of my usual smock. Though it wasn't supposed to rain, without a moon, there was no way to tell how cloudy it might be. Better to be safe than sorry. I pulled out a lightweight tarp and spread it over the mosquito netting. By the time I'd finished, I had a kind of tent, covered on all but the side facing St. Andrew's. I'd secured that flap in a way that could be shut quickly if needed.

One more step before getting started. I'd turned off my phone while on my date, so thought it would be a good idea to check to see if there were any missed calls or messages. I expected Hadley to touch base—she'd want to make sure neither of us
~~~

went to bed angry or upset in any way.

There were no calls, but I'd been right about my aunt. I quickly responded to her message, mentioning my date with Adam, but leaving out how badly it had gone and where I was now. Satisfied what I'd written would reassure her we were good, I started to shut off the phone when Fanny's remark about emergencies suddenly popped into my head. Not only didn't I turn it off, but after muting all alerts, I tucked it into my overalls—something I'd never done before.

With palette in hand, I resumed my rendition of the church. I laid the color on thickly, working it until I'd built St. Andrew's brick by brick—all with the proper shades to add depth and character. Soon, the entire building came into view. The stained-glass windows took shape, each color adding yet another facet of reality to the painting. I added the large firs that flanked either side of the church, set in the metal handrails as they rose from the sidewalk to the terrace at the top. But every time I tried to work on the stairs themselves, my hands would begin to shake uncontrollably. No matter what I did, I was not allowed to paint the steps to the doors of St. Andrew's.

I set the palette aside, switched off the lamp attached to the easel, and ducked beneath the mosquito netting into the open air. Though I was close to the parapet, I was still far enough away to keep my fear of heights at bay.

The thought made me laugh, thinking about how dismissive I'd been when Sean mentioned me being afraid. I'd handled the situation quite well, even if I had to say so myself. Didn't give him the inch...

Perhaps this was a good time to take a real break, make a pit stop. I snatched my license from my purse, along with a few dollars and my car keys. Though it wasn't far to the convenience store, I figured it would be better to drive than to walk this time of night. After making sure my work area was completely covered and protected, I was on my way.

Before I allowed the roof door to close, I checked to make sure the key would unlock it. I knew it would, of course, but why take a chance? Both the top door and the lower one shut securely behind me, automatically locking. It didn't keep me from testing the knobs, however. Now who was being OCD?

There were few people out, and other than the clerk, no one at the store. She appeared thankful for the company, so I stuck around exchanging a few minutes of small talk while I munched on licorice bits. When one of her friends came in, I used the restroom then headed back to work.

I didn't see another car on the road, or any people. After all the folks the police had rounded up during the curfew, this surprised me. I was able to park in the same spot as before, directly in front of the door. Before unlocking it, I took a good look around, making sure I was alone and not being followed. I'd no idea why that even occurred to me. Probably the way Adam had acted earlier.

By the time I reached the roof, my creative juices were flowing, urging me back to work. The lights from the church easily showed me the way and kept me from tripping over anything.

Was that a raindrop?

Please, God, no.

Yes, I was prepared, and really didn't need to be here to finish the painting, but it's where I *wanted* to be. Outside in the night air, where only the distant sounds of traffic filtered through the incredible peace and quiet. Whether or not the moon glowed above me, this is where I felt the urge, the overpowering need to create.

But where there's one raindrop there's bound to be more.

I made it inside my protective covering just before the heavens let loose. As the rain pelted my makeshift tent, I turned on my lamp and attacked the stairs to the church.

It was as though the rhythmic tap-tapping of the rain as it fell onto the tarp lulled me into a protective cocoon where nothing seemed impossible. One step, two, then all of them appeared like magic from my brushes. Lights and darks, a convergence of shadows, everything worked with an incredible smoothness that, by the time the shower ended, the painting was virtually finished. I signed it in the lower right corner and sat back, marveling at how quickly it had come together. There was no doubt about it; this had been a "God thing."

That's when I noticed the tiny anomalies on the bottom three steps. I'd been so busy reveling in the finished project that I'd missed something...

I unhooked the lamp from the easel, holding it closer to the canvas.

Red? Minute red dots sprinkled the lower corners of the steps directly above where I'd signed my name. First, there was confusion, then horror gripped my heart as the symbolism struck me.

It's where my mother had been shot.

I'd been running on adrenaline, the kind of high that comes when your unconscious mind takes over and allows the muse to kick in. But there was no time to question why the painting ended up this way. A sudden splash in a nearby puddle consumed my full attention. I quickly shut off the lamp at the same time I removed the painting and placed it in its protective case. Another splash, and I became as still as a statue, barely breathing, listening as footsteps came closer.

My "tent" was hit so forcefully it started to collapse. I grabbed the easel and pushed my way from beneath the falling mass. I was knocked over the second I emerged, the easel flying from my hands. A dark figure stood over me, silent, threatening in his dark-colored ski mask and hoodie.

I tried to stand but found myself being lifted into the air. I shoved my elbows backward into the attacker, hoping to hit someplace vulnerable. When that didn't work, I attempted to gouge his eyes. At least one of my fingers hit the mark. His grip lessened enough that I was able to break away.

With only the lights from the church across the street to guide me, I ran in the direction I thought the easel may have landed. He wasn't far behind.

He grabbed the neck of my sweater, choking me as he drug me toward the parapet. I couldn't stand, but there *was* something I could try.

Flailing my arms, and by the grace of God, one of them finally made contact at his most vulnerable point. He snuffed, growling in pain as I took advantage of being set free. Still on my backside, I grabbed him between his legs and squeezed. While he was momentarily incapacitated, I took off in the opposite direction, scrambling over the roof on hands and knees until I finally found what I wanted.

I didn't wait to stand. Instead, I rolled over just as the man got into range. I swung the easel at his legs, hitting him so hard the easel broke in half. I barely made it out of his way when he went down, his head smacking against the roof. I backed away, watching, waiting for what his next move might be.

But I wasn't alone: I had 9-1-1 on the line.

Chapter 18

I'd stayed on the line until the walls of the stairwell blocked the signal. From the moment the police pulled me out onto the sidewalk, things took on an otherworldly aspect. The flashing lights, sirens, people seeming to all speak at once... Too much input after the experience I'd just had.

There were no signs of an intruder—no pry marks on the doors or anything to indicate he'd entered without a key or my having let him in. It's not that they didn't believe something happened, my condition was proof of that. They just didn't think I was telling the whole story.

I sat for awhile in the back of a patrol car until the chatter on the scanner became too much to bear. The officers outside the car were so busy talking about a drug bust earlier that evening to even realize I wanted out.

My hands were evidence. Tucked beneath the nails might possibly be DNA or another clue. They used what they called a hinge lift on my clothing, letting me know the sticky tape could collect everything from a latent print to fibers and other trace particles—much better, I was assured, than having them take my clothing into evidence. I understood but didn't understand when they said I couldn't have any of my equipment—not even my painting. For the time being, it was all part of a crime scene.

What did the perpetrator look like? Are you certain of the height, the weight, that you didn't see his face? I repeated the answers by rote: 5'10" or 11", about five inches taller than me; maybe 200 pounds—stocky but not fat. What part of his face being covered by a ski mask didn't they understand?

Did I want to be checked by the EMTs? When I refused, insisting I was fine, they whisked me away to the station and placed me inside the same room I'd been in the last time I was here. It was all so surreal and hard to process.

Why would anyone try to hurt me? I had no idea, no answers to a question I'd been asking myself from the moment the attack began.

Had I taken anyone up to the roof for a liaison? That seemed to be their conclusion. A date gone bad. Had to be something I'd done.

I knew they were watching me and didn't care. Let their profilers and psychologists analyze me all they wanted. I knew what happened.

Finally, the door to the room opened, only no one came in. I could hear voices, one of which I recognized.

"Hey, good job out there tonight. Understand you tackled one of the dealers."

"Yeah, we both went down hard. He just didn't come back up right away." They laughed.

"Neither did the reporter you both landed on."

Again the laughter.

"Couldn't have happened to a nicer guy." There was some mumbling before the door opened further and Detective Adam Davies walked in.

I don't know what I expected, but it wasn't him rushing over and taking me into his arms. Was that even allowed in here? And what about that two-way mirror? What did the cops behind it think of this unprofessional behavior?

The second those things entered my brain they were whisked away by six magic words: "You ready to go home now?"

~~~

Before taking me home, Adam took me by the ER to be checked out. He made it a condition of springing me. Any attempt of thwarting him by suggesting this was blackmail was met with a harsh glance. I decided it would be better to go along than fight. I'd had enough fighting for one night.

The doctor gave me something for my skinned hands and offered me a script for lorazepam to help calm me down enough to sleep. Though I wasn't crazy about the idea of being drugged—even a little—sleeping sounded really good right now.

"What about nightmares?" I asked.

The doctor looked surprised by the question. "Are you prone to nightmares?"

Not wanting a reason for him to pursue the subject, I shook my head. "Just worried the meds could exacerbate the experience I had."

He accepted my statement, but Adam appeared
~~~

skeptical. He didn't confront me, simply drove me back to the Gradys', reassuring me everything would be all right.

I'm glad I'd held onto my keys instead of returning them to my purse, since it and the rest of my belongings were still part of the crime scene. By the time we got to the house, I'd retrieved the keys from one of the many pockets in the overalls and had them at the ready.

Adam walked me to the door, waiting patiently while I struggled to unlock it. Once open, he stopped me long enough to kiss my forehead before turning to walk away. I called out a belated "thank you" to which he responded, "Get some sleep."

And that's exactly what I did.

Chapter 19

I awoke to what I perceived as pounding on my door. My initial reaction was to ignore it, but the sunlight peeking under my eyelids changed my mind. The westerly sun filled the room with light, telling me two things: I hadn't closed the blinds and curtains, and it was late in the afternoon. Neither surprised me.

Fanny waited at my door, a concerned look on her face.

"We thought it a good idea to check in on you. I'm sorry I had to wake you to do that, but..."

"No, don't be silly. It's fine." I yawned. "What time is it?"

"Nearly three. We heard you come in around five—"

"I'm so sorry."

"Not to worry. Emma and I are early risers. I just wanted you to know that Detective Davies had your car delivered a few hours ago along with a message that your property had been processed, and you should check with him when you've got the chance."

"Thanks for letting me know." I was happy about my car, disappointed it could take longer for the rest of my stuff.

"I'm glad you're ok, Kelsey. We heard what happened to you this morning." She shook her head. "That sort of thing just doesn't hap—*shouldn't* happen here. At any rate, Emma said to tell you that she'd love if you'd come down to the garden and visit—if you're up to it, of course."

"You didn't notify Hadley..." I let the sentence hang, the thought of my aunt being told about the incident too much to bear.

"I wouldn't. And Susan won't, I promise. She stayed in Columbia with some friends and won't be back till tomorrow. I doubt she's even aware. Perhaps it would be best if you took care of speaking with your aunt now, just to be on the safe side."

I nodded. "Please thank Emma for the invitation. I'd love to join her. It might take awhile."

"She'll understand." Fanny smiled. "She's really taken with you, Kelsey. I love seeing her this way."

"Thanks. And, Fanny, *thank you* for what you said the other day about keeping my cell on. I remembered you talking about emergencies, and, well, instead of turning it off like I usually do, I muted it. Might've saved my life."

Her face lit up so much she practically beamed. We exchanged a hug, Fanny giving me an extra squeeze before letting go.

"Take your time, sweetheart," she said, wiping a tear from her eye. "We'll be in the garden when you're ready."

After she'd gone, I located the overalls I'd worn the night before—and would never wear again—to retrieve my cell. I discarded the garment in a trash can after removing my license and thoroughly checking all the pockets.

I downplayed the attack to Hadley, assuring her I was fine, and the police were actively pursuing the culprit. I knew she didn't really believe my version but neither did she demand I return home. Instead, she declared that she'd be coming to Seaton as soon as she could make arrangements at work. Nothing I said would dissuade her, and I finally gave up trying. I'd played the "I can take care of myself" card one too many times for her to buy. Especially after what just happened.

By the time I joined Emma and Fanny in the garden, I'd accepted Hadley's decision even though I didn't like it. The women were inside the screened-in patio.

"A little buggy after this morning's showers." Emma wrinkled her nose. "Much better here. Now, let me look at you."

"Other than the scrapes on my hands, there's not much to see. I'm sore all over, but it's not as bad as I thought it would be. I just can't figure out how the intruder got up there." I took a seat next to them and gladly accepted a glass of tea. "Even though I knew the doors closed and locked automatically, I checked them to make certain no one could get into the stairwell. Director Hanson will be furious!"

"Positively apoplectic." Emma chuckled. "But don't worry about Ron Hanson, Kelsey, I've already spoken with him." She grinned. "The man likes to throw his weight around, but he knows on which side his bread is buttered."

"Emma helped get him appointed director as a favor," Fanny explained. "He's more of a figurehead than anything, doesn't know the first thing about running the place."

Fanny excused herself to start dinner, leaving me alone with a still chuckling Emma.

"I hate to admit it, but she's right. Ron's an old family friend. He'd retired too early and needed something to keep him occupied, so I suggested him to the board."

I nodded, not really listening. "There's got to be another key."

"Which is precisely what I told Ron. At any rate, he won't bother you about what happened as long as you don't try to use the roof again."

"I won't. Promise. Besides, I finished the painting of St. Andrew's just before..."

"Your physical altercation. That's wonderful news. I hope you'll show it to me."

"I'll be happy to the moment the police give it back. All my things. Except for the easel. I broke that when I hit the guy's legs."

"Sounds like you gave him something to think about. Good for you!"

"Yeah, thanks. I can't get the how out of my mind. Or the why, for that matter."

A blue jay called out from nearby. I could tell Emma was trying to locate him."

"Look, over there," she pointed. "Look how magnificent he is. He's so bright and distinguished with all his feathers preened to perfection. Do you think he worries about how he's going to find a mate? Of course not! Why not, you may ask? The why is obvious: he already knows he's gorgeous."

"I—if that's supposed to be some kind of an analogy, I don't understand."

Emma gently patted my arm. "It wasn't meant as one, but let's see if we can use it. Um... You're a very attractive young woman, all alone on a dark night. The perpetrator sees you and figured out a way to get to you."

"To throw me off the roof? Because that's what he'd intended. Would have to be a homicidal maniac." I shook my head. "It doesn't make sense no matter how I look at it. No wonder the cops didn't believe me." I got up to pace. "And now Hadley's coming! I'm sorry, Emma, I'm not very good company."

"Nonsense, girl. It's my explanation that's faulty. Come back and sit with me. That's it. Don't let this incident make you crazy, Kelsey. Don't allow that jerk to get into your head. I'm sure it was a drug addict looking to rob you. It happens even in Seaton. Why, when we got the award, the addicts stopped breaking into houses and businesses and started mugging people. That's why the council set up the curfew."

"Maybe you're right. I heard about a bust last night." We sat for awhile in silence, watching as the male jay was joined by a female. It didn't take them long to fly off together.

"If you'd like, I could call your aunt, let her know how you're doing and that I'm looking out for you."

"I don't think that would be a good idea. But thanks. I'm glad I took Fanny's advice and called Hadley before Susan did. I'd hate to think how she'd have reacted."

"Especially with Susan's penchant to over-dramatize," Emma agreed. "That Susan," she shook her head. "She was a wild one, always getting into trouble, not wanting to go to school or work like her sister. Their parents worked for us, were good friends to boot. Fanny would come and help her mom with the cooking and cleaning. We offered both girls jobs, but Susan would rarely show. Always off doing something else. Gave her parents fits. Why, she got pregnant when she was around fourteen. Luke and I helped her parents find a nice home for unwed mothers. Paid for the whole thing." Emma stared out across the garden. "We were told the baby was stillborn, broke everyone's heart. When Susan came home, she was quiet and subdued. She buckled down and finished school with good grades. She showed so much potential that Luke and I offered to pay for college."

"Wow! I'd no idea she'd been through so much."

Emma nodded. "She'd changed, became responsible. She didn't think twice about leaving college to come home and help out after Sean was born.

What was this? "But he always called Susan mom."

"I can understand your confusion, Kelsey. He grew up calling her Momma Sue and Fanny momma. It seemed like the thing to do. Fanny was so sick those first years, we thought we'd lose her."

"That explains why they're all so close." I was still trying to digest this new information. "Did my family know?"

The question seemed to jump-charge Emma forward, back to the present. "I'm sure they did."

Then why didn't I?

"Now, speaking of my grandson. He's a bit under the weather, so to speak. Not sick or anything—"

"Let me guess. He's the reporter injured in last night's drug bust."

"Yes, well, he wouldn't like me telling tales out of school. Anyway, we spoke about you using his deck to paint, and he said you should come over any time. He'll actually be in residence for awhile."

"Wonderful." Or it would be if I had enough replacements for the things the cops commandeered. I did a mental inventory of what was in my room. Paints, brushes, several canvases, and a tabletop easel. It just might work.

Besides, what could be better than starting a new painting to get over the trauma of the night before?

Chapter 20

"So, Fanny's your mother."

"Hello to you, too." Sean hobbled to meet me, a crutch under his right arm. "I see Grem loaned you the putt-mobile."

"To bring your supper. Wait, did you say "Grem"?"

He nodded. "Short for Gremma. She made it up. Cute, huh?"

"It is. Just sounds a little odd coming from you." The slam wasn't lost on him. Beyond his usual smirk, he didn't respond.

I hefted the picnic basket out of the passenger seat of the "putt-mobile," glancing up the long flight of stairs to a porch.

"That's a lot of steps. There another way in?" I assumed there must be, considering he didn't seem too steady on his feet.

"It helps keep the riff-raff out." He snickered. "And, yeah, there's another entrance." He motioned me to a door near the end of the wide bay of garage doors. "There's an elevator to the apartment. Luke and Gremma had it installed for my other grandparents."

"Your other—Fanny's and Susan's parents lived

here?" I was totally confused.

"Grem didn't tell you? I thought you must have my entire life history by now." He opened the door for me. "It appears you've bewitched my poor grandmother."

Less than five minutes with the man and I was ready to drop off the basket and leave. I controlled the urge, keeping in mind how concerned Fanny and Emma were for him.

"Don't go getting your panties in an uproar, Kelsey. It was meant as a compliment." He pressed the button for the elevator, and it opened almost immediately. He indicated for me to go in first but realized the act of chivalry was a bit misplaced when the door nearly shut on him.

"There's something you should know," he said when the elevator began its ascent. "Hadley and I spoke a little while ago."

"You *called* her?" I shouldn't have been surprised by his audacity but was. "What made you believe you had the right—"

"Whoa, there. She called me. Look, Kelsey," he hopped around until he faced me. "We're close, ok? She needed a sounding board."

"And?"

"Long story short, I recommended she stay home, told her how well you handled yourself."

When the door opened, Sean quickly hobbled through and then used his crutch to keep it open for me. He pulled a metal gate across the elevator and locked it.

"It always made Grammy Lane nervous that someone could just walk in unannounced. She felt a lot more secure after this was installed."

I totally understood. I'd wondered the same thing.

We came out at the back of a nicely updated kitchen and dining room. A row of windows brought in plenty of light and the high ceilings made the space seem even larger than it was. The main house was grand; this was homey.

"All this along with three bedrooms, two full baths, a big living room, and a great deck—which is at your disposal. It's not the mansion, but it's home. Sometimes. I tend to be on the road a lot."

"It's really nice. Warm and cozy." I set the basket on the counter and unloaded the food. "Here's a note from your, er, mom. Why didn't you ever say anything?"

"About Momma Sue not being my mother?" He shrugged. "Everyone else knew, so I assumed you did as well."

"Nope." I started to put a plate of sliced roast beef into the microwave when he stopped me.

"I'm sure it's fine. Not far enough from the house to get cold." He limped over to a bar stool, sat, and pulled the plate in front of him. "Silver in the large drawer to the left of the stove. Thanks. I'm starved."

"My parents knew—that Susan wasn't..."

"Yep. Payton figured it out, which didn't make Sue very happy. But they all seemed to get over it, understood and all that. It's really not a big deal."

Maybe not to them, but Susan had still been playing "mother" even after I'd met Fanny. I thought that was odd.

"They want you to come back to the house with me after you've eaten. To keep an eye on you."

Sean rolled his eyes and immediately looked like he regretted the action. "I know how to deal with a concussion."

I raised my hands in defense. "Don't get testy with me. I'm only the messenger."

"Sorry. The invitation has already been turned down—several times. The CAT scan didn't show any problems-"

"Other than your usual smart mouth and stellar disposition."

"Of course." He grinned. "Let's change the subject, 'k? I know you're dying to learn about the apartment."

"I wouldn't say that." I took a seat at the nearby dining table. "Curious about your "other" grandparents living here."

"You should've become a reporter—that's also a compliment. Curiosity comes in handy-"

"And puts you in the line of fire when a criminal is trying to escape the cops."

"That, too. Anyway," he took a bite of roast after piling everything—mashed potatoes, peas, and cornbread—onto a single plate. "The Lanes worked for the Gradys. The garage used to be a carriage house and included a caretaker's apartment." He went on to give a brief history of the place and how, eventually, his grandparents came to live there. "Gramps was a handyman, jack-of-all-trades, and Grammy Lane the cook and housekeeper. They raised Mom and Sue here. Which is probably why the Grady boys ended up marrying the Lane girls.

All nice and tight."

"Um. So, where did you live?" I took the extra plates to the sink to wash and dry.

"In the big house. The place had separate living quarters for my dad—"

"Caleb or Saul?"

"Cabe. That's what everyone called him. Anyway, that's why the old place will make a great bed and breakfast or country inn. Way too much room for anything else. And the upkeep," he shook his head. "Not to mention how I hate the three of them living out here by themselves. It was a fun place to grow up, though. I loved the space and roaming around the tunnels."

"Tunnels?" I set down the dish I'd just dried and stared at him. "Why on earth would they have one tunnel let alone multiple?"

"Made it easier to get to the old house and back. That's what I was told, anyway. That and I was supposed to stay out of them. They were afraid they'd collapse. But once I saw Gramps exit one, I was hooked."

"I'll bet. You know, Emma thinks the remains of the old house are haunted." I put the clean dishes into the basket as he dug into his dessert—a luscious cherry pie Emma made specifically for him.

"I know. She was the driving force behind having the house demolished. No one had lived there for a long time, and once his grandparents were gone, my dad took it down. All that's left is the root cellar, and Dad said it'd caved in decades ago. Grem's been threatening to get a crew out here for years." He shrugged. "Now, why don't we go check out my deck so you can ooh and ahh over it."

He grabbed his crutch and pointed it in the general direction we needed to go. I followed him down a short hallway into the living room.

"Sue wants to tear out the wall and make this an open concept. Personally, I like the—"

I heard him speaking but was no longer paying any attention. How could I when *my* art and my father's decorated the walls, practically covering every available inch—that wasn't taken up by an enormous TV?

"How did you—*where* did you get these?"

He swore. "I'm so used to them, I didn't think. No, that's wrong." He made his way back to me. "I wasn't thinking, but it *was* time."

"Time? I threw these paintings and drawings away. Or thought Hadley did." I felt angry and betrayed. And the apologetic look on his face didn't change anything. It made me even more furious. "She said to paint what I saw in the nightmares, get them out of my head and onto the canvas. *They were supposed to be destroyed to keep the dreams from coming back.*"

"I...it's not her fault. I found them, begged her to let me have them. They were beautiful-"

"You tore one of my sketches out of my hands and told me I'd never be an artist. You were so mean and vindictive, I hated you. Now, I find my— I can't do this." I turned to go about the same time he'd taken hold of my arm. The abrupt movement caused him to tip dangerously to one side, so much so that I was forced to reach out and steady him. We were so close I felt his breath on my face.

"I can't tell you how much I regret being such a jackass. It's a little late for apologies, so I'll just say I knew, *I knew*, how much talent you had, how proud your folks would've been to see these. Look at them, Kelsey. *Really look at them.*"

They were all different variations of the same thing, a ghostly house shrouded in fog, trees with spiny branches reaching up toward a tiny sliver of a moon. Some paintings depicted shadowy figures, others a mysterious light in the distance, but each one had the same thing in common: the house depicted was a place I'd never been to—until recently.

The Grady house.

Chapter 21

I wanted to run, to pummel him. Instead, I sat on the sofa and put my head into my hands, trying to understand, to make my Swiss cheese brain come up with a solution.

How could Hadley have deceived me like this?

More importantly, *how could I paint a house I'd never seen?*

No! I refused to sit here feeling sorry for myself. And there was no way Sean Grady would get out of this with his pathetic apology. I didn't believe his story about convincing Hadley to hand over the artwork from my nightmares. He'd more likely found them and taken them without her even being aware it occurred. Nothing else made sense. After all, this was the bully from my childhood, a person who'd taken pleasure hurting my feelings and making me miserable. Why should I believe he was any different all these years later?

"I know you're in there, Grady!" The angry voice of Detective Adam Davies pierced the silence. "We have some business to take care of," he continued, followed by a line of expletives.

"Hold your horses." Sean hollered. "It'd be best if you'd stay in here," he whispered, limping back in the direction we'd just come.

Stay? Not on his life!

"Have you any idea how your stunt nearly cost us that bust?" Davies shouted. "I don't care how important you think you are, Grady, you had no business being that close—"

"Only reason it seemed that way is because you had a runner. I was behind the line and you know it."

"Why you little—"

I was in time to see Adam reach between the bars of the gate, his fists clenched.

"I dare you to open this gate, twerp. It's about time we settle this." The detective's face was contorted, and the vicious tone made me glad I'd remained out of sight.

"I've no idea what you're talking about or why you've got such a hate for me—"

"You're a pompous, entitled little punk who thinks the rules don't apply to him. I'm here to tell you you're wrong. I want your camera and memory card, or whatever you use. If you don't fork them over I'll get a warrant—"

"What, and violate my First Amendment rights?" Sean taunted, just out of reach of the detective.

Davies kicked the gate and was about to ram it with his shoulder when I came into view. Sean must've seen me as well because his demeanor changed.

"Look, man, take it easy on the gate. I'll get you the memory card, though I don't know what good it'll do you. The best shot will be the two of you landing on top of me." He hopped out of sight.

"I didn't expect to find you here." Adam Davies's tone did a complete 180 as he made the effort to rearrange his clothing and attitude.

"I *am* staying here. Well, at the house. I brought his dinner." Surely he realized there was no "unseeing" what just transpired. Still, he tried.

"Yeah, I know. I've brought your equipment. I knew how concerned you were—"

"An officer and a gentleman. Who knew?" Sean gave me the memory card to pass on to Davies. "I hope it helps." He handed me the key to the gate before hobbling away.

~~~

"I don't know how you can stand that guy," Adam Davies said, placing the last of my things into the putt-mobile.

"Habit." What else was there to say? "I really appreciate your bringing my stuff. The idea of having to replace everything was staggering."

"No need. We kept the broken easel, which you already knew about, and the tarp. The rest didn't appear disturbed. That your painting of St. Andrew's?" He pointed to the waterproof portfolio.

"Um. I managed to secure it as the man pushed over my tent. I'm anxious to ensure it's all right."

"You want to take a look now? I'd like to see the finished work." The way he said this gave me the feeling he'd already seen it.

"Nah, it's something I like to do in private. Kind of a ritual thing. Besides, until I've the chance to
~~~

live with it a few days, I won't know if it's really completed."

"Part of your process. I understand." He gently took my hands and turned them palms up. "They still hurt?"

I nodded, wondering where this was going. I didn't have to wait to know the answer. He took me into his arms.

"Now I know why it bothered me so much to leave you last night. I must've sensed something."

It was nice in his arms, feeling the steady beat of his heart—until I recalled the scene I'd just witnessed.

"I'm ok," I slowly came out of the embrace. "Really."

His hands cupped my face. "I'm here for you, Kelsey Carol. Remember that."

I wasn't likely to forget.

Especially the kiss.

Chapter 22

There was no conscious thought involved in doing what I did next. I needed to return the gate key and pick up the picnic basket—I didn't, however, need to take the portfolio with me.

Sean called for me to join him in the living room, saying he wanted to show me something he knew I'd appreciate. He raised his expressive eyebrows when he saw the folio, but didn't say anything. Instead, he led me to a section of the room that held about a dozen of my father's photographs. Most were of various places around Seaton, many of which I'd never seen before.

I stopped in front of one that had obviously been taken just as the sun rose.

"Daddy loved getting up early to take his photos. Mom called it waiting for the magic—the time when the sun's first bloom gives everything a kind of ethereal quality." I shook my head, marveling at the photograph, how beautiful the old building looked. "They'd take me with them to share the experience. But as much as I loved spending this special time with them, I could never see what they saw. Over the years, I've continued trying to discover their morning magic. Never have." I moved from one photo to another, surprised by his collection.

"Thank you, Sean. I needed this." I wiped a tear from my eye, hoping he hadn't seen.

"It's called the golden hour. It's a window of time right after sunrise and before sunset. I soaked in everything your dad said like a sponge."

"I didn't... I remember now. Whenever you came to visit, you were always begging to go out with them. It made me jealous that you saw something I couldn't, that somehow you were better than me." Ok, that was way more than I intended to say. But I couldn't help myself. The memories of those times were so clear I felt if I reached out I could touch them.

"And I was jealous of you." He gave a little laugh. "I was fascinated by their talent and would've given anything to be in your shoes."

"No. No you wouldn't. Because then you'd have to live with the belief that if you'd gone with them to shoot the church that morning that maybe they'd still be alive. That the monster who killed them might..."

"What?" He turned me toward him. "Decide it wasn't worth killing a kid as well? That's nuts, Kelsey, and you know it. If you'd been on those steps," he stopped abruptly, removing his hand from my arm and carefully backing away.

"You know something about that day. Don't you?" Now I was the aggressive one.

"There's a reason why you don't recognize these photos. Some of them are your parents', some mine."

Without meaning to, I'd backed him into an overstuffed chair. He landed with a thud that brought a look of pain to his face.

"I-I'm sorry. Really. I just need you to stop beating around the bush and spit it out. Tell me what you know—*what I don't know!*"

"I wanted to go with your folks that morning. It drove me crazy that they'd take you even though you didn't want to go—when that's *all* I wanted." He lowered his head. "Hadley had driven up the night before."

"I don't understand. Hadley and I came to Seaton *after* they were killed."

"No, Kelsey," he said, staring directly into my eyes. "You were already here, staying right here in the apartment."

I felt behind me, knowing the sofa had to be nearby. I almost fell onto it.

"That's not possible. It's not—that's why the paintings of the house are from this direction. But-" I refused to cry, refused to allow anything to keep me from learning the truth.

"Anyway, I got up early and waited in the garage until they'd driven away. Then I snuck up here and swiped Hadley's keys—"

"Your "fond" memories?"

"Not that time, no. But it wasn't the first or the last time I'd borrowed her car."

"You were what, fifteen?"

"Um, yeah." He swallowed hard. "Would you mind getting me a bottle of water?"

"You can drink all you want when you're finished." I matched glare for glare.

"You're hard."

"And you need to quit stalling."

"Ok, you win. But you're going to wish you had a bottle by the time I'm done.

"Anyway, I got there within seconds of the shooting, heard a vehicle speeding away. I parked in the middle of the street next to your parents' car, totally unable to take my eyes off those steps and how the blood..." His hands shook where he held onto the arms of the chair. "I had the camera your dad gave me around my neck and remembered how he always said, "you'll recognize the shot when it comes." I started snapping off pictures, one, two, three. That's when I saw you plastered against the back passenger window. Your eyes were so wide, fixed on the carnage in front of you. I knew I had to get you out of there, away from the scene before anyone found them—found us. I was amazed at how easily I convinced you to get into Hadley's car. You followed directions, but you weren't there. You were lost somewhere I couldn't reach." It sounded like the description Hadley had given me.

"I drove like a bat out of hell, passing the paper delivery truck blocks from the scene. Hadley was waiting, ready to have me punished for stealing her car. Then I told her what happened, what you'd seen. With you out of it like you were, our only thought was to protect you at all costs. That's when we devised the plan to keep you from remembering."

"And it worked. You should be proud of yourselves." I'm sure the irony of the statement was lost on him.

"We were. Until you returned to Seaton, demanding to meet the only person who'd seemed to stir the public conscience in the last twenty years."

"You're S. Pattison?"

"Yep. And from the moment Grem told me about the sketch, I knew you were in danger. That your memories were returning."

"Then someone tried to throw me off a roof..."

"And they won't stop until you're dead."

Chapter 23

While I got ice packs for Sean's ankle, he studied the drops of red on the steps in my painting.

"Definitely compelling," he called out. "And you're right about the placement."

"Another clue, confirmation I was really there."

I helped him with the ice then sat next to him. "Is that—is that how you remember it?"

"Can't get it out of my mind. You're sure someone at the station looked at this?"

"There's no way to know, is there? I'm making the assumption based on the way Adam behaved. Guess I've got a suspicious nature."

"You need it. Especially after that sketch—now this. If the wrong person saw it—"

I shivered. "We should have moved this discussion to the deck. At least we'd have the sunset..."

"What's to stop us?"

In the middle of relocating, my cell rang. Emma and Fanny were worried I hadn't gotten back to them. Once we'd both assured them everything was fine, that we were just getting reacquainted, Emma made a final request.

"Since he's not coming to the house, would you

mind sticking around to keep an eye on him overnight? It'd make me feel a lot better if he wasn't alone."

"That isn't necessary, Grem. You know—"

"I'm speaking to Kelsey, young man. It's her choice," she said sternly. "Not yours."

Her concern won me over, and I consented, even though I actually agreed with Sean. Though he'd protested while we were on the phone, he seemed pleased by my decision.

Once on the deck, we sat in silence, enjoying the warmth of the evening and the stunning view. Sean made a point of letting me know when the "golden hour" of sunset occurred. And, for the first time in my life, I understood why it had meant so much to my parents.

"Are you crying?"

I ignored his question, watching as the sun began its slow descent below the distant hills. Then it was time for more answers.

"So the photo I'd seen in the paper right after the murder was one you'd taken?" He nodded. "I've searched for it, practically looked all over the state."

"Yeah? There's a good explanation for that." He readjusted one of the ice packs, moving it from his ankle to his knee. "You have to remember I was fifteen and full of myself—no comment from the peanut gallery. Even though I was terrified, it wasn't enough to keep me from wanting people to know what happened. As long as I could remain anonymous. Next thing I know, Hadley's calling, demanding I get that picture back *immediately*. I'd no idea how to do it, of course, but knew from her voice I had no other choice. So, I mentioned to Gremma how much I'd like to learn about newspapers."

"She got you a job at *The Seaton News.*"

"More of an internship, I guess you'd call it. I was only there about three days when I found the original and the plate. Destroying them was a highlight of my teenage years." Sarcasm dripped from the last statement.

"And the negative?"

"Kept in a safe place, waiting till I could find someone trustworthy enough... It was so much bigger than what might happen to you or me—I knew that whoever killed Miles and Payton had been trying to keep their own secrets from being discovered."

I took a gulp of water, swallowing hard, the implication of what he'd said startling me into a new awareness. "You believe my parents might've inadvertently taken a photo of some kind of criminal activity."

"Yes, I do. Why else would the killers take their cameras and film bags?"

"What about the items police have in evidence?"

"My sources say all they have is a camera they found in the trunk of the car and a couple rolls of film—developed, of course. Those are mostly buildings and fields, no people."

Once more, silence ensued. Between the two of us, anyway. My brain was a totally different matter. Revelations were wonderful but were still tempered by the truth behind the saying that every clue brought more questions than answers.

The last of the birdsong sounded shortly after the sun sank over the horizon. Tree frogs chirruped along with the occasional cricket. Stars dotted the dimming sky, the only light during this phase of the moon. Our conversation seemed incongruous to our surroundings.

"You know, I'd asked you to dinner last night so I could reveal my mysterious alter ego. You can imagine my surprise when I saw you with Davies."

"Why do you despise him so much?"

"In case you didn't notice, it's mutual." He removed the ice from both his knee and ankle then rubbed the areas. "It all goes back to the day he and a couple other cops came into the paper asking for that photo. I'd nabbed the things but hadn't gotten them out of the building yet. I don't know; maybe I acted suspicious or maybe he just didn't like my face. Whatever it was, from that moment on he's tried to find reasons to give me a hard time." He grabbed his crutch to help him stand. If he could've paced, he would have.

"You know he went on a bunch of your parents' shoots."

I nodded. "He said I should recognize him. I'd no idea what he was talking about."

"Well, there was something about that relationship that suddenly made Davies big man on campus. Even the detectives seemed to take a backseat to him. Blew my mind."

"So you didn't feel you could trust him because he didn't like you?"

"I didn't trust him because of the way he

strutted around, taking over at the same time he refused to accept any information that disagreed with his assessment of what happened. He even managed to push around the state investigators." He might not be able to walk well at the moment, but he'd definitely figured out a way to pace. I attempted to rearrange some of the furniture so he wouldn't hurt himself.

"I know he can be harsh, but he seems dedicated."

"To himself. Don't misplace your trust, Kelsey. I'm telling you, that dude would turn on his own mother if it would advance his fame and notoriety."

"That's a little over the top, don't you think?"

He whipped around, facing me. "So would being slapped with withholding evidence or an obstruction of justice charge. I don't know about you, but I've no desire to spend time in jail for trying to protect you and find the scum sucker who killed Miles and Payton."

"Ok, Sean. I get it." I approached him cautiously, not wanting to risk knocking him over again. "How about coming over here to sit with me. You can prop your leg up and relax. No more talking. I've already enough to digest for the night." He allowed me to help him back to the wicker sofa. And when he lifted his leg to rest it on the table, I tucked a pillow beneath his heel.

"There's something I haven't told you, something that may or may not be important." His voice was eerily calm.

"Ok. You sure you don't want to save it—"

"I've been holding onto these secrets for twenty

years, Kelsey. I know it may not seem like it, but this is the first time I don't feel like I'm in this by myself. No offense. I'm really proud of you. You've taken this a lot better than I thought you would."

"Right time, right place. I've wanted answers and have also felt alone." I don't know what possessed me, but I took his hand in mine and gave it a little squeeze before bringing it up to my lips for a gentle kiss.

"But what I'm about to tell you might change your mind." He drew in a deep breath. "When I got you out of the car that day, you were clutching a canister of film. I've never known why, but you handed it to me. No prompting. By the time I got you back to the apartment, I'd forgotten all about it. Didn't remember it was in my jeans—then, I..."

His entire body stiffened. He removed his hand from mine, placing it on my shoulder instead. I could feel the tension increase as I turned to him.

"Sean?"

"There were only a couple photos on it. Your dad had given me lessons on developing pictures, so I processed them, just as he'd shown me. They were of Grandpa Luke, my dad, and Uncle Saul talking with Davies. And none of them looked happy. I couldn't figure out why Miles would've taken the photos. It was weird and didn't seem important, so I never said anything. But over the years, I've wondered how that canister came to be in your hand. Why out of all the ones in the car, you were holding that one." His pale blue eyes met mine.

Suddenly, I was thrust into the nightmare that

had haunted me all these years. A man with a crazed look in his eyes rushed toward me, his hands thrust before him, dripping with blood. *But that's not what really happened.* I'd gone to him.

I jumped up from the sofa, wanted to run, wanted to scream, but all I could do was cry.

"D-Daddy gave it to me."

Chapter 24

"How?"

The word seemed more a demand than a question. Either way, I didn't know if I had an explanation. The only thing I knew for certain was that my father had given me that roll of film.

"I d-don't know, Sean. All these years I've interpreted the nightmare as..." The words fell flat between us. It wasn't the whole story. I knew that now.

"I woke up because of the noise—gunshots. Daddy first. Bang! He went down, holding his neck. Mom had turned toward the car, shaking her head at me when the bullet struck her forehead. Maybe she was still in motion, maybe that's how the drops of blood ended up on the steps. I didn't know, don't know. She fell and some man ran over and tugged at the camera around her neck until it finally came off. She just flopped around like a rag doll." I backed away when Sean reached for me. Though I knew he was in front of me, I remained in the past, watching as the monster who'd hurt my mother began running toward me. *A gun pointed directly at me.*

"I don't know why he didn't shoot me. He was

right there. Then he wasn't. That's when I heard something that made me get out of the car."

All of a sudden I was twelve years old, asleep in the backseat of my parents' car while they set up for their morning shoot. I came awake from a pleasant dream and entered a nightmare world I didn't know how to process.

Daddy clutching his neck, Mom...

"Don't look at mom. Come to me. That's it." Daddy's voice guiding me.

"He had the canister in his hand, and then it just rolled down the steps toward me. I picked it up and ran back to the car. Even though I locked the door, I knew it wouldn't stop a bullet. But I didn't know what else to do."

Sean took me into his arms. I held onto him so tightly it hurt, bringing me sharply back from the twilight world I'd been in.

~~~

Sean told me where to find the photos that had been on the film my father had gotten to me as he lay dying. Three black and white photos of men I'd only seen, or believed I'd only seen, in other pictures around the mansion and on the internet—with the exception of Adam Davies.

"I don't understand what's so important about these that he..."

"That's what I thought. Until now. I've still got the negatives. I can enlarge them. Maybe there's something in the background."

I held the photos up to the lamp, carefully
~~~

searching each one for something, anything that would be a logical explanation why Daddy needed me to have that film.

"There's nothing here. I don't understand. Maybe it was the wrong canister. This can't have been so important to spend your last breath on."

"Unless it goes with something else they found. Some other—"

"You don't have it. Hadley doesn't have anything even remotely suspicious. And you said the stuff the cops have in evidence—"

"I know, but..."

"It's been a long night, Sean, full of discoveries and very little else. Don't get me wrong; I'm glad you came clean. It's nice to have some of those holes filled in. But I wish it hadn't come at the expense of reliving my parents' deaths. I could've lived the rest of my life without those memories." I tossed the pictures onto the coffee table. "But I haven't been, not really. In one way or another they've been haunting my dreams, my art. If I could only remember what that monster looked like!"

We tried to change the subject but kept coming back to the same things over and over again until exhaustion overtook us, and we fell asleep. In one another's arms.

Chapter 25

Something startled me enough to pull me from a pleasant dream and out of Sean's arms. My sudden movement woke him. He seemed a little dazed, looking at me in confusion.

"What?" He rubbed his eyes. "Something wrong?"

"Listen." There it was, a kind of thud off in the distance that echoed through the hills. I left his side, moving to the deck's railing. No lights, no detectible movement. "I thought maybe it was back."

"It?" He carefully maneuvered his bad leg, testing its mobility before standing.

"I don't know what else to call it—" There, a clash of metal on metal just like I'd heard a few nights before. "Could you turn off the lamp? It might be better... Ahh, the lights are back." By the time he reached me, they'd disappeared.

"You just missed them."

He stared out across the dark fields. "Missed what?"

"There were lights out there," I pointed in the general direction. "But they're gone now."

"So the banging and lights are connected

somehow?"

I nodded.

"I've got a new Nikkor 14-24mm—" he could tell he'd lost me. "It's a powerful telephoto lens perfect for night photography. If you want to get it for me, we can take a look."

He told me where to find his camera bag. When I returned, the eerie lights had reappeared. Just like the first time I'd seen them, they seemed to hover slightly above the ground with an erratic movement.

"It's at least two people with flashlights or lanterns. Here." He helped me balance the camera as I peered through.

"Definitely not ghosts," I mumbled.

"Ghosts—ah, your nightmare paintings with the floating lights. Like that sketch Grem told me about. Which would be why she told you how she felt about the remains of the old house." He took another look, snapping several shots before lowering the camera. "I think someone's using the root cellar."

He moved away from the railing and began putting away the camera and lens, handling each piece with the same tenderness my father had used with his equipment.

"I think we should investigate," he said, bringing me back to the present.

"And how do you propose we do that? You've got a bum leg, and I'm out of easels."

"Cute. Neither of those matter because we've got something they don't—"

"The tunnels?" I stared at him, incredulous. "You said they'd caved in."

"That's what my grandfather said." He asked if I'd take the camera bag back into the house. He followed close behind. "I explored them quite extensively—"

"Recently?"

"I was maybe sixteen, seventeen."

"You've got to be kidding. You've no idea what shape those things are in. It'd be insane." I put the bag onto his couch and watched as he retrieved a knapsack from a closet and started loading it with a smaller camera, flashlights, and water bottles. "You're not kidding."

"It's what I do. Or prefer to do. Investigating, instead of sitting behind a desk, is a lot more interesting."

"And your leg?"

"Practically healed." He took a step without the aid of the crutch, attempting to prove his statement. His wince didn't convince me.

"Why don't we just call the police and report—"

"No." The sharpness of the answer brought me up short. "This is my property, and I'm going to find out what's going on. You can come if you want, up to you." He headed down the hallway. "I'm going to make a pit stop and then head out. There's another restroom through there. If you're coming, I suggest you use it." Was this bad Sean again or just his naturally stubborn nature? Either way, I couldn't let him go alone.

~~~

It's not how I wanted to spend the rest of the
~~~

night, but the first half hadn't exactly been planned either. I'd always insisted Hadley see me as strong and independent, able to take on anything life threw at me. I'd just never thought it would end up being so much in so little time. The ironic twist was the fact I actually felt even tougher and more determined than I'd claimed.

But not quite enough to go along with Sean's harebrained scheme. Yet, that's exactly what I was preparing to do.

Sean and I made certain our cells were on, programmed with each other's numbers to dial with a single touch. He left messages for Fanny and Emma—just in case something unforeseen happened.

"They need to know where to find us," he said, then reassured me it was only a precaution and everything would be fine.

He still used his crutch, insisting it was more for a weapon than because he actually needed it. He then armed me with a baseball bat to replace my "weapon of choice." After rechecking the items in the knapsack, we were on our way.

Despite it having been so long since he'd last used the tunnel system, he had no difficulty finding the concealed door from inside the garage. He shoved several concrete blocks against the door to hold it open before we walked into the darkness.

"It's wired—or was, anyway." His flashlight scanned the walls that were surprisingly made of bricks and concrete.

"It looks like a basement—but a lot more narrow." I'd expected it to be damp and smell bad, and it did a little, but not as much as some old basements I'd been in.

"Wide enough to bring in the booze." He laughed. "I think my great-grandparents had the place re-wired and shored up. But you can tell the original builders took great pains to make the place secure. Only the best for the Grady's bootlegging operation." He continued his search of the walls. "Ah, let there be light."

About every other bulb appeared to be out, but enough worked to reveal the arched concrete roof and walls. Some areas of the floor were cracked and broken with patches of dirt and roots—I hoped that was all—but it wasn't even close to what I'd thought it would be.

"We go down a few steps before going forward. There's no telling what shape they're in, so be careful."

"I was about to tell you the same thing."

He turned back to me, a big grin on his face. "This is an adventure, Kelsey. You said you were ready for something different."

"A lighter discussion, yes. Not some crazed-reporter-type stunt that could... Exactly how far back does this go?" The bulbs hanging from the ceiling seemed to go on forever.

He shrugged. "I'm guessing a mile or so. Maybe more." He pushed forward, sometimes balancing with one hand on the wall for extra assistance while using the crutch.

Something scurried by me, making me cringe, but I didn't say anything. Sean was bound and determined to keep going, and there was no way I'd go back by myself.

To keep my mind off what might be in here with us—of the four legged variety—I decided it was a good time to ask him a few personal questions.

"Tell me how your parents decided on your name. All the other males had names from the Bible."

"In short, they thought Mom was dying, and my dad wanted her to choose my name. So, I was named after her grandfather. When Grandpa Luke found out, he was furious, insisting Grady's had chosen Biblical names for generations and that wasn't about to change." He stopped and turned back to me. "He couldn't believe his youngest son dared to go against tradition. Didn't matter that Sean is another version of John, it was unacceptable. Even when my dad made my middle name Luke, he wouldn't accept it—or me. My uncle sided with his father. Needless to say, I never got along with either of them. No matter how Gremma tried to diffuse the situation, it never worked."

"I'm really sorry. You think that's why Susan held you so closely? Was she trying to spoil you to make up for their rejection?"

"I don't know," he said, pushing onward. "At first, it seemed like a favor. Then, I went because I loved your family. Besides, I had an adoring mother and father, two wonderful grandmothers, and a doting aunt. Gramps made sure I learned things he thought I should know, seemed proud of me. All this to say I didn't really feel the slights of Luke and Saul. The one I felt sorry for was Dad. He was a great guy, loved to read and work with his hands.

You'd have liked him."

The further we went, the more cracks appeared in the floors and walls. We'd been in the tunnel about twenty minutes when Sean stopped cold.

"We're almost there," he said, breathing heavily. "There's a bit of a rise before it flattens out again in front of the root cellar. The key for the door is on the lintel."

"Unless someone's put on another lock." Which seemed logical to me. If you were up to no good, you'd want to make certain to keep people out.

"Unlikely. Even if they knew about the tunnels, they wouldn't necessarily know where the door is or how to open it. As I said, the key is on the lintel. It's kind of a trigger that activates the spring latch." He slowly lowered himself to the floor.

"And why are you telling me?" I had a bad feeling about this—if it were possible for this "adventure" to feel worse.

"I've got to rest awhile."

"Fine. I'm in no hurry." Which wasn't true. I really wanted to go back the way we'd come.

He shook his head. "You go on, get inside. Snap a few photos, then get out of Dodge. By the time you get back, I'll be good enough to make the trek home."

"This isn't some *Scooby-Doo* mystery, Sean. And we don't separate!"

"No, it's not. But it *is* important, Kelsey. To you, as well as to me. You saw the strange lights out here twenty years ago, and they disturbed you enough to have nightmares about them. Enough to put them into your paintings."

"But there was a monster out there," I said, reminding him of the terrifying figure in the sketch Emma told him about.

"Which I'm sure represented the guy who came at you with the gun the day your parents were killed."

"You're even more irritating when you make sense." I pulled my cell from my pocket and checked the signal strength. There wasn't one. "Nothing. You?"

He shook his head. "Nada. Just get in and out as fast as you can."

He showed me how his small 35mm worked, put it back in the knapsack, and removed one of the flashlights.

"Remember, in and out. And make sure you stay out of sight."

"Right," I said wryly. "Like I'm going to yell or wave my arms around to get their attention."

I was a few steps down the passageway when I realized he hadn't told me how to open the door from inside the root cellar.

"I never closed it."

"You never... So, what are you suggesting?"

"Find something to keep it open."

Chapter 26

The first thing I noticed when the door clicked open was the light coming from the root cellar. Was that good or bad? I figured I'd find out soon enough.

I slipped through the opening, making sure to stay low to the ground. Once through, I searched the floor for something to place in front of the door. Though the area was full of stuff, none of it was small enough to keep the door and passageway from being noticed should anyone enter the room.

I crawled forward, popping up now and again to get the lay of the land. Someone was using the space as a bedroom. There was a rusty iron bed with a thin mattress which was piled with blankets and clothing, boots on the floor, and a chemical toilet in one corner.

A shuffling from the adjacent room, along with angry voices, stopped me in my tracks. There were two men arguing, one blaming the other for a botched attack—the one on me the night before.

"All you had to do was throw the little bi-"

"Yeah, blame me. You weren't on that roof. The girl was tough."

"Really? She's what, about a hundred ten,

hundred fifteen pounds soaking wet?" The gravelly voice taunted. "You allowed her to get away. Crawled back here to lick your wounds."

"I don't have to take this!" A stocky man came into view. His hands were clenched into fists at his sides.

"Hate to tell you, bub, but you do. It's either that or go back to prison. Right now, you're gainfully employed, to a degree. You're off the streets, which is more than you can say before I found you."

"I ain't no killer," the big man said, pushing out his chest. "Which is more than you can say."

"True. But you're on the sex registry for—"

"Enough!" The man stomped into the room where I hid. "The girl said she was eighteen. Not my fault." He slammed his fist into a cardboard box inches from my head. "I'll deal for you, but don't ask me to kill again."

The other man entered the room. Outlined by the brighter light from the outer room, and from my position on the floor, he seemed a bit taller than the first guy. Maybe around six foot. Unlike the first man, he appeared clean with a well-trimmed beard and close cropped hair. He, too, had a stocky build, or perhaps it was just the clothes he wore.

"You will do what you're told, understand? Remember the agreement."

If the stocky man hadn't chosen that moment to sit on the bed...

"Looky what we have here. A little rat sneaked in when we weren't looking." I was grabbed by my hair and yanked to my feet, the bat flying from my hands. "Did you get all that, sweetheart?"

I refused to meet his eyes, refused to show fear."

"Get her bag, Randall. Let's see what the rug rat brought with her."

The knapsack was ripped off my back at the same time the "boss" shoved me toward the toilet.

"Water, flashlights, and a camera." Randall threw the items on the bed. "I don't get it."

"I do, bub. Means we've another rat in the tunnel." He turned toward me, leering. "Now, don't you go anywhere, sweetheart. Me and Randall have plans for you." He ordered his partner to tie me up.

My hands were forced behind my back, but I didn't make it any easier for him than I had the night before. Only this time, he had help.

I continued struggling, kicking and flailing my arms until the "boss" pulled what looked like a hunting knife from a sheath around his waist. That's when I saw Sean rush into the room. His crutch came down on Randall's head, causing the man to crumple to the floor. The "boss" pulled me in front of him, holding the knife to my throat.

"You might want to rethink your next move, 'cause I won't think twice about cutting her."

Sean put the crutch down, his eyes never leaving the man's face. He looked like he'd seen a ghost.

"Saul?"

Chapter 27

Gravelly laughter filled the room. I was shoved toward Sean, the knife nicking the skin on my throat.

"Finish tying your girlfriend up, reporter, and make it snappy. If you try anything, I'll slice you first and then finish her off nice and slow. You wouldn't want that now, would you, lover boy?"

"This is your uncle?"

"No talking! Tie!"

Sean shook his head, then cocked it downward. I tried to look, but the blade of the knife prevented me from doing so.

"Anyone else in that tunnel?" The boss asked as Randall groaned.

"No."

"So you thought you'd rush right in and save her, huh? How's that working for you?" The man checked Sean's knots. Satisfied, he pushed me onto the bed and indicated for Sean to tie my ankles.

"Is that really necessary?" Sean stared directly into the boss's eyes.

From my position, it was possible to study the man as well. And it *wasn't* a man. The realization was both stunning and alarming.

"Susan?"

The hand holding the knife not only remained steady but came closer to me.

"Now why'd you have to go and do that? We were getting along so well." She said, remaining in character.

Randall moaned again and was answered by a swift kick in the head.

"You move, Sean, and she bleeds out before you're able to get help."

He stood where he was, a little wobbly without his crutch. As he leaned forward to take hold of the bed frame, Susan nicked my throat with the tip of the knife. I could feel a trickle of blood leaving a trail down the neck of my t-shirt.

"What part of don't move do you not understand?" I couldn't see her eyes, but her voice was deadly serious.

"I'm sure you'd have preferred I fall over, but I thought my last moments would be a little more comfortable this way."

"Always the smart mouth, huh, kid? Or is it you don't believe I'll kill her?"

"He said you were a murderer." Probably not the best segue, especially when she seemed intent on doing me bodily harm. And who could blame me for choosing the wrong words? Just trying to wrap my brain around the rough-voiced man actually being Susan had my head spinning.

"Saul was, but I'm guessing you already know that, S. Pattison. Don't look so surprised; with all I know about you, it wasn't hard to figure out."

"I didn't think about my family outing me."

Sean shifted his position slightly only to have Susan threatening to cut me again. He raised his hands to prove he wasn't making a move on her.

"So, you took over the "family" business."

"Drug trafficking is such an ugly term, don't you think? I prefer to consider it an entrepreneurial venture. Poor Kelsey looks lost."

I considered the woman before me, the wig, beard, men's clothes, and thick-soled shoes to add stature. How could the round little woman I knew have shoved me so hard I'd flown across the room?

"I'm freakishly strong."

"How'd you—"

"Know what you're thinking?" She cackled. "*Please*. I've known you your entire life." She stared down at me, disgust oozing from her.

"All those years, the concern, it was a lie?"

"Ah, don't cry now, dear," Susan switched from the gravelly voiced persona to the one I thought I knew. "Things will be better real soon. I promise."

I felt the gall rise in my throat. "And the invitation to stay here, to ease Hadley's concern?"

"All an act. I'm good." The self-satisfied smile was only partially hidden behind the fake beard. "I had to keep an eye on you—both of you. I knew Sean would end up telling you what he knew about the murders. It was only a matter of time till your memory returned. That stupid sketch proved it."

The sketch. The strange man running toward me, his clawed hands dripping with blood...

"You were in disguise then, too. You shot my mother—"

"Technically, that was Luke."

"You had a gun pointed at me."

"Would've shot you, too, but the guys insisted we get out of there. As it happened, you were so freaked out you lost your memory. But I stayed vigilant, continued the relationship with you and Hadley, making sure Sean was always in tow. You two were like oil and water, constantly at one another's throats. Then, anyway."

"So what now, Momma Sue? You arrange an accident for Kelsey and me?"

She'd raised her eyebrows in feigned surprise at his use of the endearment. She reached out and pricked his arm with the knife. "Worked before. Only this time, I don't think we'll kill you first."

I was lost again, but Sean seemed to know exactly what she was referring to. "That's why Dad's body was never found. Well, your plan didn't work that great; it killed Saul, too."

"You're already dead, Seany boy, so I'll satisfy your curiosity. When your dad figured things out and threatened to go to the cops, Saul staged the accident. He made sure he got out of the truck quickly enough for an easy swim to shore." Her eyes twinkled. "With Cabe six feet under and Saul presumed dead, we were home free. The perfect plan and execution. He hid out here and was able to continue conducting business as usual—with my help, of course."

A scuffling from the direction of the tunnel caught her attention. When she turned toward the still open secret door, I took the opportunity to kick her, connecting with the hand holding the knife with enough force that it sent the weapon flying. Sean lunged at her, pinning her to the floor. Just as she screamed, Detective Adam Davies dashed into the room, his gun drawn.

"Thank God," I cried.

But the next words chilled me to the bone.

"One move and I'll put a bullet in your brain."

ALICE K. ARENZ

Chapter 28

"There's my baby boy!" Susan squealed, shoved Sean aside, and used his head for leverage to jump to her feet. She retrieved the hunting knife before sidling up to Davies.

"Cut it out, Susan. We don't have much time." He kept the gun trained on Sean, appearing to enjoy this turn of events. "Wake Randall and get the rest of the product loaded. The charges are set, and we need to be gone from this location immediately."

Susan frowned. "Is that any way to treat your mom?" She mumbled, coming to the bed and taking one of our confiscated water bottles. She poured the water into the face of the unconscious man and prodded him with her foot.

Without turning his back on us, Davies closed the door to the tunnel and then sprayed something around the edges that smelled horrible.

"He's sealing us in," Sean whispered.

Davies responded to the remark with a twisted grin.

Meanwhile, Randall struggled to stand, shaking his head till it looked as if his eyes would pop out. He protested being rushed until Susan mentioned the charges. That did the trick. Within seconds, both he and Susan disappeared into the other room.

"You're blowing the tunnel?" Sean, still on the floor, inched closer to me. I'd finally managed to sit up, all the while working to get free from the ropes around my wrists.

"Enough to destroy several sections without causing more than a slight depression above ground. When we're finished, this place will become your tomb. Fitting, don't you think, with your father buried not far from here?"

I could tell the taunt made Sean want to charge Davies. Who could blame him? Thankfully, he controlled himself—which seemed to irritate the detective.

"So, I'm guessing you're the baby that didn't actually die at birth."

Adam Davies gave me a measured glance. "See, I knew you were smart. Just not enough to stay away from this piece of garbage."

The rigidity of Sean's shoulders spoke volumes. I touched him with my foot, trying to diffuse a situation that could only lead to him getting shot.

"I'm assuming your name's no coincidence. A sort of beacon that you're a Grady."

"Unlike your boyfriend here, my mother held to tradition."

"With the exception of your last name," Sean growled. "Let me guess, one of Luke's dalliances. And with a child. You should be so proud."

Davies holstered his gun. The intensity of the snarl on his face frightening.

He was across the room and on Sean in a blink of an eye. He kicked Sean in the gut, then lifted him by the shoulders and punched him squarely on his nose. The crunch that resulted told me it'd been broken. Before Sean had a chance to react, the detective—former detective?—slugged him in the abdomen so hard, the whoosh of air from his lungs put him down for the count. Davies threw him aside like the sack of garbage he'd claimed Sean to be.

"This what you did to my dad?" Sean's voice was barely above a whisper.

"Worse, kid. I beat him to death. He was as big a coward as you are." He got back into Sean's face, held him by the hair, then laughed when Sean flinched. "There's something to be said for going all Biblical. After a lifetime of abuse, killing my step-brothers brought more gratification than I thought possible. Killing you," he said, drawing closer to Sean's face. "Will be icing on the cake." He patted Sean across the cheek, slapped him, then let him go. That's when his eyes focused on me.

"You chose the wrong side, Kelsey. It's a shame, but that's the way it's got to be." He stroked my hair. "He'll come around long enough to keep you company while you suffocate. If I didn't cause him too much internal bleeding."

He strode out of the room, barking orders to his underlings. I heard a lot of movement, sounds of footsteps on creaky steps, the squeak that would come from the overused wheels of a shopping cart—or one of the handcarts I'd invariably get at a big box store. Once they'd emptied the room of their cache, they intended to bury Sean and me alive—sealed forever in what remained of the cellar.

At least Emma would have her wish; the remains of the old house would finally be destroyed.

It was a strange thought but one that offered a glimmer of hope. *Emma and Fanny would know where we were.*

Please God, have them find us in time.

Chapter 29

Where's the safest place to be when the explosions started? I didn't know, but tied up and sitting on that thin, lumpy mattress wasn't the answer.

The moment activity in the outer room ceased, I was on my feet, searching for something, anything, to help remove the rope from my wrists. I nudged Sean, trying to bring him to consciousness. Being knocked out twice in twenty-four hours couldn't be good. He needed medical attention. But first, we had to get out of the cellar.

"Wake up, Sean!" I hollered as I ran into the outer room. It was filled with tables made from sawhorses and sheets of plywood—all of them empty. Old shelving along one wall still contained an errant canning jar or two with heaven only knew what sealed inside.

"Like we'll be if you don't wake up, Sean!" I wasn't screaming, but close.

I checked every shelf, every nook and cranny, found a couple gallon-sized bags with what I guessed might be marijuana, but nothing capable of cutting the rope.

A muffled boom along with a ground tremor said we were running out of time. I ran back to the other room, colliding with Sean. Blood streamed from his nose, and his eyes were slightly glazed, but he was awake and aware of what was happening. He dragged the mattress behind him with one hand while the other held his knapsack.

"The doorway." He yelled as another boom shook the ground beneath us.

We huddled close together beneath what should be the strongest point in the cellar, the thin mattress over our heads. Sean managed to untie my wrists just before a third charge went off. This one nearby.

"That's the entrance to the cellar," Sean said, hugging me tightly against him. "It'll block the root cellar from the outside. I'm betting it's the last of the charges."

The lights flickered and went out.

"It's ok, Kelsey. I've got the flashlights, and we still have a couple bottles of water. I'm sure Mom and Grem felt something at the house. Even a little tremor would be enough to wake them."

"And if they're awake, they'll likely check their phones." He nodded. "*If* they felt something. Davies said they'd collapse the tunnel without causing damage above ground. Perhaps-"

Another softer boom, with only a slight movement of the ground, spoke of a charge from further away. The ground may not have shaken much but the cloud of dust particles filling the air was concerning. We both began to cough.

"We've gotta get out of here before we choke to death!" Sean tossed aside the mattress and searched the knapsack for a flashlight. He gave it to me while he dug in his pocket for his phone.

"Did they take your cell? Mine's toast."

Despite all the pushing and shoving I'd endured, the protective case on my cell had done its job. The phone worked but there was still no signal.

"Nothing."

"Plan B," he said, struggling to his feet. "Were you able to tell which directions the explosions came from?"

"I think the first two were behind us. In the tunnel. Next was the one up front, and the last one..." I shook my head. "I'm not sure."

"That's good enough for me." He turned on the other flashlight and limped over to the wall without the shelving. He began methodically feeling the wall, going from the floor to as far as he could reach above him. Each time he stretched upward, there was an imperceptible groan.

"What are you doing?"

"That way's the old entrance to the cellar. The back room had the secret door to the tunnel we came through."

"Right. Your point, Sean?" My impatience led to a coughing fit. He stopped his search and got me a bottle of water.

"Sip, Kels. No gulps." He went back to what he'd been doing.

"You ever see *National Treasure*?"

"Sure. I love that movie. What has that got to do-"

"You remember me telling you there were tunnels?"

"Sean!"

"Well, just like the Masons had a secondary way out in the movie, the bootleggers had one as well. I know it's in here, just not *where* it is."

"That's why it has to be in one of these side walls!"

I flew to the shelving units, determined they were coming down. Yes, they were heavy and awkward, but that wasn't about to stop me. Sean yelped when the first unit hit the floor, causing something from the shelf to fly off and hit him in the back of his legs. When I tugged on the next unit, he was right beside me, helping. When it toppled over, an irregularity in the wall proved to be the secondary door we were looking for. And getting it open wasn't as hard as we'd feared.

We shined the flashlights into the blackness. The beam highlighted hundreds of thick cobwebs that made me cringe. The air was stale but better than what we'd been breathing.

Before beginning our journey, I went to find Sean's crutch. It hadn't survived the blow he'd given the thug Randall, but I had another idea up my sleeve.

"The bat?"

"You'll hold onto me and use the bat as a cane. It'll work." It had to.

The scenario didn't give either of us a free hand to hold a flashlight. While Sean tried to figure out a way to get it to work, I made a last-ditch effort to get us out of there. I shined my flashlight onto the cement and brick walls, searching for a light switch. Even if I found one, the chance of the electricity being on in here when it was out in the cellar was slim to none. But I didn't give up the hope—or my prayers.

Though I'm sure it hadn't taken as long as it seemed, I finally located the old push-button switch. Another fervent prayer, and I pressed the button, praising God when the lights came on—weaker, with fewer bulbs, but on, nonetheless.

"Must be a separate line." Sean's amazement and thanks for my persistence was rewarding. I could tell he was flagging, had no idea if we'd reach the exit before he passed out, but I was determined to try.

I attempted to keep him talking. The guy who never seemed to shut up would have none of it. He moaned louder with every step we took. Within minutes, he was barely able to move. He dropped the bat, and not even the clanging sound it made when it hit the concrete registered. I tried to drag him, but he was too heavy. I finally lowered him to the floor, my tears hitting his face.

"Sean?" I gently moved the hair from his forehead and kissed it. His breathing was labored. After forcing a little water down his throat, I wet the corner of my t-shirt and wiped his face, careful not to touch his poor nose.

"You gotta go on, Kelsey. Bring back help." He slumped to the floor.

After what seemed an eternity, I emerged from the tunnel through a narrow opening in the grove of trees next to the Grady's garden. The place was lit up brighter than I'd ever seen it. Even though it was late at night, early morning, the garden was alive with activity.

Emma spotted me first, calling the state police and EMTs to my location. I told them everything I knew about Sean's injuries and showed them how to get into the tunnel. Though I wanted to go back with them, Emma and Fanny insisted I stay behind. I gave the women as many details as I could about what happened to us, then promptly collapsed into Fanny's arms.

Chapter 30

They loaded an unconscious Sean into an ambulance, allowing his mom to accompany him to the hospital. A Missouri Highway Patrol officer offered to take Emma and me there as well.

"I want you checked out thoroughly, Kelsey." She patted my hand. "You're a hero, sweetheart." She held my hands the entire way to the hospital, regaling me with the events that led up to my emergence from the tunnel.

"After what you and Sean had gone through the night before, I couldn't sleep. I didn't want to disturb Fanny, so I went out to the screened-in porch on my own." That's when she heard the strange thuds and metal on metal sounds and saw the lights. "I knew immediately that it came from the area of the old root cellar." She'd had her suspicions about what might be going on, but it wasn't until the first charge went off that she'd picked up her phone to call the authorities.

"That's when I saw Sean's message about the two of you going into the tunnels. I'd no idea what he was talking about. But, it scared me to death! I called the Highway Patrol and suggested they get in contact with the DEA, FBI, and anyone else they thought was appropriate. I was still on the phone when several more explosions occurred." Which made the authorities eager to get to the Grady's property as soon as possible.

"Fanny joined me in the middle of my call. She was terrified for you and Sean. She'd been in the tunnels as a child. She and Susan used to play there until their father put the fear of God into them. I'd no idea something like that existed, though with this family's history, I shouldn't have been surprised."

By the time we reached the hospital, Sean was already in surgery.

"He's got internal bleeding," Fanny cried. "A lacerated liver, damage to his spleen, and who knows what all." I took her into my arms, assuring her Sean's stubbornness would see him through.

The three of us prayed for Sean—and that the authorities would apprehend Susan, Adam Davies, and their associates sooner rather than later. That's when we found out the pair had been in the DEA's sights for some time. Despite Davies's and Susan's careful planning, they'd not been the smart super-criminals they thought they were.

"We started checking into Davies's background and the cases he'd been involved in. Things just didn't add up. And when we questioned one of the dealers we'd taken into custody, he claimed Saul Grady was the boss and was backed up by a Seaton police officer. We knew we had to get inside that organization."

Hadley arrived at the hospital accompanied by a state investigator. We were escorted to a private room where I learned how my aunt had taken a box from the apartment twenty years ago—never believing it to be anything more than some of her twin's personal items—a diary, family photos and such.

"It wasn't until I talked with Sean last night that it even occurred to me there might be something of importance in the stuff." She wrung her hands. "I was so worried about protecting you from memories of what you'd seen and of the loss of Miles and Payton that I just shoved the box in the back of a closet and forgot about it."

As much as I wanted to know about the contents of that container, it wasn't going to happen. Instead, the investigator wanted me to tell him everything I remembered from that day twenty years ago. I gave him as detailed a description as I could, adding the information about the sketches and paintings I'd done following the murders—the nightmares that were far more real than I'd ever guessed they could be.

"I need to speak with Mr. Grady as soon as he's well enough. We're beginning to get a picture of what really went down that day and hope to be able to share our information soon."

When he'd gone, Hadley and I went back to the family waiting room, anxious to get an update on Sean's condition. A few minutes later, the doctor and a nurse came to speak with us.

"We were able to repair his liver and save his spleen. He's badly bruised inside and out, so it will be awhile till he's back on his feet."

"He won't like that," Fanny remarked, her voice shaking. "That boy's never been able to sit still.

Always has to be doing something."

"I'm afraid he won't have much choice, Mrs. Grady. He has to give his body a chance to heal—which will help his leg as well. I've told him to stay off it."

"And his nose?" Everyone turned to look at me like I was an alien or something. "Davies broke it when he slugged him in the face." There, that should explain... absolutely nothing.

"It's all taken care of. His black eyes and taped-up nose will give him bragging rights." The doctor smiled at me. "He's going to be fine. We'll just want to keep him in the hospital a few days."

We took turns sitting at his bedside, waiting for him to wake up. It was Fanny and Emma who got to speak with him first.

"Other than wanting a hamburger and a chocolate shake, he wanted to make sure you were ok." Fanny grinned. "And he asked about you first."

Throughout the day, members from different agencies brought us news on the investigation. The interrogations of Susan and Adam Davies sounded like a freak show.

Though taken into custody still dressed as a man, Susan went into her flighty, endearing little woman act. When she realized they weren't buying it, she broke into tears, claiming years of abuse at the hands of Luke and Saul Grady had turned her into the criminal she was today. Fear that they would somehow return from the dead and harm her was the reason behind her nefarious activity.

She had no idea Sean and I had survived, nor did she realize her son, now ex-detective Adam

Davies, was already working on a deal with the prosecution. *If* he could manage to cut through all the lies and actually tell the truth.

While the interrogations continued, investigators from various agencies walked the property, studied the secondary tunnel system, and ultimately found the graves of both Caleb and Saul. What Davies didn't know about setting explosives would come back to haunt him. Bullets taken from both bodies matched the rifling on the bullets taken from my parents. And since his sons had been killed six years after his death, Luke was immediately ruled out as a suspect.

Emma and Fanny gladly gave agents permission to take any and all guns on the property, both in the main house as well as from Sean's apartment and the garage. Combined with search warrants for Susan's suite of rooms and Davies's apartment and his adoptive parents' home, they found a treasure trove of evidence.

Three days after our ordeal, Sean was ready to check out of the hospital, whether they wanted him to or not. What he hadn't counted on was the four women who backed the doctor and nurses rather than him.

"You're not going to win this one, Sean, so you might as well capitulate." I told him. "I didn't help save your life for you to throw it away by being stupid."

"I seem to recall things a little differently, Miss Carol. Weren't your hands tied behind your back-"

"By you."

"Yes, but at the direction of weird Susan who

was wielding a rather nasty knife."

"True."

"Then I got us beneath the doorframe during the explosions."

"Don't forget the mattress."

"I haven't."

I smiled at him and received a rather pathetic, cockeyed smile in return. They might be black and blue, but he still had the most remarkable pale blue eyes I'd ever seen.

"Thank you for saving my life." He said solemnly. "I think in some cultures that means I belong to you."

"Really? That's rather over-dramatic, wouldn't you say?" I stood next to his bed and took his hand and squeezed it.

"To the contrary, my dear Miss Carol. I think it's quite appropriate under the circumstances."

"And those are?"

"I've been in love with you since you were thirteen and you told me in no uncertain terms to shut up and grow up."

"And I've been in love with you since you saved my life when I was twelve. I just didn't know it until a few days ago."

"So, you're still trying to one up me, huh?"

"Sean." When his eyes were fully focused on me, I leaned toward him till our lips were nearly touching. "Shut up and kiss me."

~~~
~~~

JUSTICE AFTER MORE THAN TWO DECADES!
S. Pattison

Susan Grady pled guilty in court today to the murders of Miles and Payton Carol twenty-one years ago this week. There was overwhelming evidence against her, including a ballistics match to a gun she'd stolen from her father-in-law, Luke Grady.

Also charged is former police detective Adam Davies. Though it is uncertain what role he played in the Carols' murders, he has taken a guilty plea in the murders of brothers Saul and Caleb Grady, having used the same weapon that killed the Carols.

Both Mrs. Grady and Davies are still facing several federal charges, including drug trafficking and distribution.

Charges are still pending in the kidnapping and attempted murder of Sean Grady and his wife Kelsey.

THE END

OTHER BOOKS BY ALICE K. ARENZ

The Wedding Barter
Romance

Riley Carr has been best friends with Amy Lawton since they were toddlers. While Amy awaits her discharge from the Army, Riley's been left in charge of helping to arrange "a very small, intimate ceremony with no fanfare" for Amy and her fiancé. But, Riley has something else in mind.

With the aid of two other friends, Riley presents her "wedding barter" idea to groom, David Herron. He agrees, providing best man, Mike Todd, stays in the loop to keep things from getting out of hand.

It doesn't help that the giant of a man is threatening, overbearing, and just doesn't seem to like her or her ideas. But, when Todd gives Riley an ultimatum of producing results in three weeks or he'll take over, she's determined to prove him wrong. . .in more ways than one.

Portrait of Jenny
Romantic Suspense

Not even a beautiful woman can save Richard Tanner from his past.

Following an explosive—and public—argument with his ex-girlfriend, artist Richard Tanner races into a rainstorm, gripped by a powerful migraine. He wanders to the gazebo in University Park, where he meets the beautiful and mysterious Jenny—a brief encounter that leaves an indelible impression on his mind—and in his paintings.

When Detective Jack Hargrave accuses Richard of the brutal assault on his ex, he finds himself confronting demons of a past he doesn't remember. A time when little Richie Tanner walked into University Park whole, was beaten and left to die…a time that may hold the key to his future.

An American Gothic
Mystery/Romantic Suspense/Gothic

She came to Foxxemoor to write a mystery, not to become part of one.

Devastated by the death of a child in her care, Lyssie's heart strings are tugged when she finds another child in danger. Amid past secrets, lies, and betrayals of an old college friend's family, she must choose a twin brother to trust. If she makes the wrong decision, she could not only lose her own life, but also the life of the child she's come to love.

The Case of the Bouncing Grandma
Book 1 – The Bouncing Grandma Mysteries
Cozy Mystery

Has Glory hit her head one too many times, or was there really a foot dangling out of that carpet?

Reduced to watching new neighbors move in as a form of amusement, Glory Harper is stuck in a wheelchair with a broken leg, bored, and itching for some excitement. She just doesn't expect it to come in the form of a foot dangling out the back of a carpet as it's carried into her new neighbor's house. The problem is getting someone to believe her.

The moment police recognize Glory as the woman whose misadventures have given her a sketchy reputation, her believability quotient lowers considerably. Just when she thinks someone's taking her seriously, Glory realizes Detective Rick Spencer, a Harrison Ford look alike, appears more interested in her than in her story.

But, while she's looking in what seems the obvious direction to solve this mystery, the real criminals are hot on her trail.

The Case of the Mystified M.D.
Book 2 – The Bouncing Grandma Mysteries
Cozy Mystery

First a foot, now a hand—what body part is next?

When her puppy finds a severed hand on a walking trail, Glory Harper is positive the signet ring belongs to a missing college professor who caused a lot of trouble around town before his disappearance. Her insatiable desire to solve the mystery of his murder finds her in over her head with a community filled with secrets, blackmail, and arson.

With her sister Jane overwhelmed by trouble with her fiancé and an arson fire in her home, Glory latches onto an unlikely partner, and soon feels as though she's stepped into an episode of the *Twilight Zone*—where nothing is as it appears, and danger lurks around every corner . . .

Including from her boyfriend, Detective Rick Spencer.

Mirrored Image
Classic Romantic Suspense

Their faces were the same, will their fates be as well?

Eccentric newspaper columnist Cassandra Chase and by-the-book Detective Jeff McMichaels clash over the murder investigation of Lynette Sandler—a woman who looks eerily like the popular columnist.

For McMichaels, the Sandler case becomes more than a test of his mental acumen. Despite departmental regulations and his own common sense, he finds himself drawn to a woman he was determined to dislike. While he and the department are hunting a murderer, Cassie sees the uncanny similarities between her and Lynette's lives as a reason to launch her own investigation—and what she uncovers gives her the sneaking suspicion that she, not Lynette Sandler, was the murderer's original mark.

She just needs to stay alive long enough to prove it.

SHORT STORY
Mystery
Home Cookin'

The new, beautiful little subdivision of Serenity View isn't all it's cracked up to be—unless you're talking about the sheetrock, driveways, or foundations of the houses! There's more hidden behind the walls in these houses than skeletons in the proverbial closet. But home builder and contractor Bubba Payton has met his match. And when he's found dead in his prized pecan grove, there are more than enough suspects…maybe even the crows that live in the grove!

ABOUT THE AUTHOR

Alice K. Arenz has been writing since she was a child. Her earliest publications were in the small, family-owned newspaper where her articles, essays, and poems were frequently included. A member of American Christian Fiction Writers, Arenz is a Carol Award winner and two-time finalist. She writes "clean" fiction as well as Christian fiction in a variety of genres and lengths. Visit her at her web site: www.akawriter.com